Totally Bound Publishing books by Rose C. Carole

Anthologies
His Domain: The Auction

Kitchen Confessions

CATERING TO HIS DEMANDS

*Dear Jennifer,
Enjoy a taste of the whip!
xoxo
Rose C. Carole*

ROSE C. CAROLE

Catering to His Demands
ISBN # 978-1-78686-360-7
©Copyright Rose C. Carole 2018
Cover Art by Melody Pond ©Copyright May 2018
Interior text design by Claire Siemaszkiewicz
Totally Bound Publishing

This is a work of fiction. All characters, places and events are from the author's imagination and should not be confused with fact. Any resemblance to persons, living or dead, events or places is purely coincidental.

All rights reserved. No part of this publication may be reproduced in any material form, whether by printing, photocopying, scanning or otherwise without the written permission of the publisher, Totally Bound Publishing.

Applications should be addressed in the first instance, in writing, to Totally Bound Publishing. Unauthorised or restricted acts in relation to this publication may result in civil proceedings and/or criminal prosecution.

The author and illustrator have asserted their respective rights under the Copyright Designs and Patents Acts 1988 (as amended) to be identified as the author of this book and illustrator of the artwork.

Published in 2018 by Totally Bound Publishing, United Kingdom.

No part of this book may be reproduced, scanned, or distributed in any printed or electronic form without permission. Please do not participate in or encourage piracy of copyrighted materials in violation of the authors' rights. Purchase only authorised copies.

Totally Bound Publishing is an imprint of Totally Entwined Group Limited.

If you purchased this book without a cover you should be aware that this book is stolen property. It was reported as "unsold and destroyed" to the publisher and neither the author nor the publisher has received any payment for this "stripped book".

CATERING TO HIS DEMANDS

Dedication

To my wonderful editor, Ann Leveille,
whose careful guidance helped hone this work for the better.
To my many friends in the romance community who offer their support and encouragement. I would never have published without you.

Chapter One

Sam needed a drink. It was kids' night at the club—none of the men she usually scened with at the Playground were there, and most of the ones available were far too young for her. Her days of scening with men in their twenties and early thirties were long over, so she probably wasn't going to play this evening.

At least she'd been able to congratulate Mya on receiving a permanent collar from Jake, and from the looks of things at the spanking bench, Mya and Jake were celebrating with gusto. She was happy for them. She hadn't believed Jake would ever commit, and she'd given him a hard time, but now that he and Mya were really together, she could back off.

Rebecca, her partner in the company Catered Affairs, waved at her from the bar, and Sam was grateful Rebecca and her Dom weren't engaged in a scene so she didn't have to drink alone. That would have been an open invitation to the baby Doms wandering around, and she just wanted to relax and talk if playing wasn't an option. But as she approached, she realized that

Mike Lyons was included in the group standing with Rebecca. *Damn!* He always threw her off balance. She changed direction in an effort to find other people to drink with, but Rebecca shook her head and didn't let her get away with it.

"C'mon, Sam, join us!" she insisted, motioning with her hands for emphasis.

Sam sighed in resignation and headed over to Rebecca, who was standing with her Dom Ethan, Allegra, who worked with her and Rebecca in the kitchen, and Mike, a P.I. who was a friend of Ethan's.

"We were just celebrating Mya's collar," Rebecca informed her as she approached. "What'll you have? Ethan's buying."

"I'll have a white wine. Doesn't look like anyone I want to play with is around tonight, so I guess I can go alcoholic."

Mike turned without hesitation and his attentive gaze locked on her, preventing her from looking away. A scar went from his right ear across his neck and disappeared into his shirt. One would assume it made him unattractive, but it only added strength of character to an already handsome face. Deep blue eyes above high cheekbones complemented his sandy hair and ruddy skin—deep blue eyes that bored into her own, rooting her to the spot. Her mouth went dry, her pulse quickened.

"I'd be glad to scene with you, Sam. I've wanted to for a long time," he offered, his voice low and seductive.

Her better judgment warred with her desires. She hesitated long enough for Mike to take it as an invitation to approach, intercepting the white wine from the bartender and placing it on the bar. "I'd like you completely clear-headed when we play."

Crap! What the hell is going on with me? She was usually able to cut him off at the pass, before he could even suggest scening with her, but she had left herself open with both her words and her actions—or lack thereof. "I'm not sure," she hedged. "I think I'd just like to stay and talk with my friends."

Mike moved in closer, his looming, well-chiseled body both a threat and a promise. "I don't think you wore that lovely corset just to stand around and talk," he observed. "It's time to give me a chance, Sam. We've been circling each other for quite a while."

Sam looked at her friends for help, but they were conveniently ignoring her. Annoyance with Rebecca, who knew she was intimidated by Mike, flashed through her then dissipated. Rebecca thought Mike was just the kind of Dom Sam needed and had encouraged Sam more than once to play with him. She couldn't be mad at her, but she didn't agree either.

"I don't want to insult you, Mike, but I don't think we'd be compatible." She reached for the wine, but Mike sidestepped so she couldn't get it without pushing him aside.

"Why not, Sam?" he asked in a soft voice, creating an intimacy between them that shut out everyone else. "I have a good reputation here. I'm careful and considerate of the subs I play with. I would never hurt you, at least not in a way you wouldn't want. And I'm excellent with a dragontail, which I know you like." He smiled at her with that beguiling grin that made her squirm.

He was right. She loved the feel of the dragontail licking at her flesh. But he'd left out the important part—he wouldn't just whip her the way she wanted, he would demand she give herself over to him, to truly submit, not just her body but also her soul. She didn't want that and he knew it. Why couldn't he just leave her alone to play the way she wanted to—have fun, no commitments? Some of the Doms called her a 'do-me sub', but she didn't care. They sure were willing to play with her anyway, and when they pushed for more she called her safeword and walked away.

Mike was different. She'd seen him play and knew he didn't let the women he played with relax and let him do all the work. He enticed them to engage through his sheer force of will. He made them shatter, then he put them back together again. She didn't want to shatter for anyone. She needed to maintain control at all times.

"Your hesitation to answer tells me you want to but are afraid."

His statement pulled her out of her thoughts and further raised her ire. "I'm *not* afraid. I just don't want what you're offering," she retorted with barely suppressed anger.

"What am I offering besides a dragontail scene? I don't think I mentioned anything else." Again with the grin, except this time it was veering into a smirk.

She was caught without an answer. The battle inside her waged—the temptation of having the kind of scene she really craved versus her fear of letting go, particularly with a Dom who would take all she had. He just stood there, waiting, watching her try to figure out what she was going to do. In her heart she knew he was already in control. He continued to regard her with laser focus and she couldn't look away. Finally, she capitulated to the inevitable. Why, she wasn't sure.

"Okay, I'll do it," she told him, ambivalence seeping into her words.

"Not good enough," Mike countered. "I'd like to scene with you, but I won't have you halfway. The answer is 'I'd like to play with you, Sir'."

Of course it is. All in or not at all, exactly what she'd been afraid of. She rolled her eyes in frustration and blurted out the dreaded phrase, "I'd like to play with you, Sir."

He grabbed her firmly under the chin, forcing her to pay attention.

"I will not tolerate disrespect, Sam. No eye-rolling, shoulder-shrugging or evasions. You will answer my questions honestly and verbally. Punishment will be swift if you try to push me. Am I clear?" His blue eyes raged, taking on the color of a stormy sea.

Riveted to attention, her nipples peaked and her clit hardened. She could barely prevent a moan from escaping her lips. "Yes, Sir," in a soft voice was all she could manage. He continued to hold her chin, watching her closely until he seemed to decide she got the point.

"I'll get you some water and we can go into the play area." He turned to order from the bar, but two bottles of water appeared in front of him. Sam glared at Rebecca, who had been the benefactor of the water. She just winked back.

"Follow me," Mike instructed. He picked up his toy bag and walked off with the clear expectation she would follow him. She did.

Mike was a little dumbstruck. He couldn't quite believe he had been able to convince the elusive Sam to play with him. He had been watching her for a while, enchanted by the way her bountiful flesh responded to the lash. She was a force of nature — confident, beautiful and definitely submissive, if someone were ever able to tap into that side of her. He wanted to be that someone.

He picked out an empty St. Andrew's cross and walked over to it, forcing himself not to look back to see if she was following. The moment he revealed any uncertainty, she would wrest control back from him. He needed to be vigilant. Once he placed his bag on the floor near the cross, he slowly turned to regard her, folding his arms over his chest. She approached and stood rigidly in front of him, crossing her arms, meeting his gaze with a defiant look. *Nope, that will not do!*

"Eyes down, hands at your sides. I'm going to remove your corset."

He didn't move until she obeyed him. Then he crowded her, invading her personal space, stroking her arms as he circled her. He leaned in and spoke very softly.

"Safeword?"

"'Red' will do."

He let her lack of proper address go for the moment. "Anything I need to know? Health issues, triggers?"

She shook her head. He gripped her arms and pulled her against him, then placed his lips against her ear. "Okay, my dear, here's a further explanation of my rules. No talking except to answer my questions *verbally*, and the answer will always have 'Sir' attached. No head shakes or any other forms of nonverbal communication. Am I clear?"

Her whole body stiffened, and he could feel the fight rage inside her before she surrendered with a quiet but definite, "I understand, Sir."

"Good girl." She trembled at his words. Whether it was because she was annoyed at him or that her submissive self was responding only time would tell.

He stepped back and began to unlace her corset. She stood still as a statue, and by the time he had it loose enough to remove the front hooks, her breathing had become shallow. As he ambled around her, once again lightly stroking the firm flesh on her arms, she remained with her gaze down even when he stood in front of her.

"Good girl," he praised again and she tensed. He didn't care—he would force her to acknowledge her submissive nature at every opportunity. He opened each hook on her corset one by one, running his fingers between her breasts and down her torso as the delectable orbs were revealed. Her breath hitched delightfully, calling his cock to respond. And it did, unable to resist the tasty morsel in front of him. He placed the corset on the table near the cross then turned to admire her luscious body. She was thin but with graceful curves, her small waist flaring out to deliciously rounded hips.

"You're beautiful, Sam."

Her cheeks flushed and there was a minute shift in her shoulders as she straightened. Her breasts were full and pendulous, more than a handful, with large dark areolae surrounding now-pebbled nipples. *Hmmm. Already turned on despite herself.* Reaching out, he rolled one of her nipples between his fingers, causing her to bend toward him. Gripping her firmly around the waist, he forced her upright, kissing her gently on the lips.

"Uh-uh. Don't move, Sam. No matter what I do, don't move."

Silent, obedient, she tolerated him as he enjoyed the beautiful bounty of her breasts. He leaned over, sucking a nipple into his mouth, enjoying her slight sigh in response. She had no idea how exquisite she was when she let herself go—her dark eyes wide, her breath hitching, her lips slightly parted. He could feast on her breasts for hours, listening to her delightful moans of pleasure.

As he enjoyed her, the only thing that stirred was her chest as she took deep breaths. She remained stock-still as he'd demanded, provoking him to challenge her self-control. He couldn't help it. Pushing her was more fun than he'd anticipated. Grasping her nipple, he squeezed it hard, eliciting a strident moan. *That a girl!* Suppressing a smile, he moved on.

"I'm going to take off your skirt now," he warned. He walked back around and lowered the zipper on the red latex mini, allowing it to fall to her feet. Now it was his turn for shallow breaths. She wasn't wearing panties, and the lush twin globes of her ass were outlined by red silk garters holding up lace-topped red stockings that traveled down her shapely legs to her shiny red stilettos. *Yes. Very nice.*

Holding her by the arm, he instructed her to step out of the skirt. Silently she obeyed his command. He couldn't resist palming her ass and squeezing hard, ending with a firm pinch, forcing out a hiss of air, but she didn't complain. Hiding his grin behind her back, he walked over to his bag and pulled out two leather cuffs.

"Hands," he instructed. She immediately presented her right hand and he secured the cuff around her wrist, then he raised her palm and kissed it. Her eyes flew up to his and her brow furrowed as though she couldn't understand his affectionate move.

"I appreciate your compliance, Sam. I felt the need to express it."

"Okay."

He didn't release her hand and just waited her out. Her pretty blush was its own reward.

"Okay, Sir."

"Thank you for your manners. You'll get the hang of it." He winked.

A flash of defiance crossed her eyes, but she didn't voice her annoyance. *Progress.*

"Let's have the other hand."

Without hesitation she presented her left. He attached the cuff and kissed that palm. She didn't react this time. He retrieved two more cuffs and secured them around her ankles. As he rose, he skimmed the insides of her legs with his hands, removing them just before he reached her pussy. Her muscles clenched, but she didn't react otherwise. He knew it was all she could do to stay still.

"You're doing so well, Sam. I'm proud of you."

She shuddered then relaxed, but not before he realized the shudder was indicative of suppressed exasperation. *Too bad.* He would continue to force her to connect emotionally as well as physically, whether she liked it or not.

"Now I want you facing the cross."

She sauntered toward the apparatus, languidly placing her arms above her head and resting her head against her arm in a subtle act of rebellion. *Not having it!* Securing her arm cuffs to the cross, he pressed himself against her as he insinuated his knee between her legs, roughly kicking them apart. Her body rose to attention. *Better.* But he knew she was going to challenge him every step of the way. He could handle that. In fact, he welcomed it.

Remaining firmly against her, he reached around and grabbed her breasts, squeezing hard. Sliding his hands down till he reached her nipples, he fondled them for a moment then pinched them forcefully, eliciting a gratifying gasp.

"I think these would look very nice in my new Japanese clover clamps. Don't you agree, Sam?"

Her hands balled into fists, but she answered, "If you wish, Sir."

"I think I do." After retrieving the mean device from his bag, he rounded the cross to face her. Her shoulders hunched as if she were steeling herself against the pain she knew was coming. To throw her off-guard, he caressed one breast then bent down and licked it gently, swirling his tongue around the nipple over and over until her shoulders relaxed and she was squirming.

"Sensitive here?" he teased. "Could you come just from nipple play?"

She continued to squirm but remained silent.

"I asked you a question, Sam. I expect an answer."

"Fine. Yes. I can come from nipple play... Sir!" she added hastily.

"Bordering on disrespectful," he warned as he stepped back and attached a clamp.

Her chest caved in as she attempted to deal with the pain. He stroked her cheek as he instructed her, "Breathe. Relax against the pain. Don't fight it."

"Easy for you to say. When was the last time someone clamped *your* nipple?" she snapped.

"You just crossed the border. No warm-up for the second one." He placed the second clamp on her distended nipple and stood back.

"Fuck!" she screamed.

"Settle down or you won't like what happens," he told her calmly. "Or use your safeword." And he reveled in the fact he'd gotten an impassioned response.

Dammit! He was pushing all her buttons just like she'd known he would, and she didn't like it...or if she were honest with herself, maybe she did. No one dared challenge her like this in the dungeon. She usually negotiated what kind of impact play she wanted and Doms gave it to her without forcing her to become emotional about it. Now, as she lost control to Mike, she gained something else. A new feeling—of being subjugated to a force greater than herself, one she couldn't manipulate. She could relax, giving herself over to a power that would lead her on a new adventure.

Without thinking she raised her eyes to look at him. His stance was combative, waiting for her next countermove. She bent her head and lowered her eyes in a gesture of submission.

"Yes, Sam. I will take care of you," he assured her, his whole demeanor changing. He lifted her chin so she could look at him, his gaze soft, his smile genuine. "I treasure your submission. I do not take it for granted."

"Thank you, Sir."

He planted a tender kiss on her forehead. "I'm going to warm you up with a flogger before I give you the pain you crave."

He didn't wait for an answer. Reaching once more into his bag, he withdrew a bullhide flogger and the dragontail. He laid both of them on the table next to the cross. Moving behind her, he began gently slapping her shoulders, slowly moving down her back to her ass, where the smacks got firmer. She rocked back and forth to the rhythm of the slaps, enjoying the skin-to-skin contact.

"I want you to stay still now. I need to know that I'm going to hit where I'm aiming."

She nodded and he pinched her ass.

"I mean, yes, Sir."

"Good girl."

She closed her eyes and gave herself over to him, relaxing her muscles to absorb the force of the blows. She felt the flogger strands tease along her shoulders, down her back, then strike her ass. *Mmm, yesss.* She usually couldn't get off from a flogger—she needed more pain than it delivered—but she liked how it settled her, preparing her for a more intense whip. As Mike traversed her back and ass with the tails thudding against her muscles, ending with just a bit of a sting, a need blossomed for more. The pain from the clamps had dissipated somewhat now that she had gotten used to them. When they came off it would be another story, but at the moment, she craved a bite of pain.

As if he'd read her mind, Mike suddenly reached around her and pulled on the chain connecting the clamps. A jolt of agony traveled through her body, awakening every nerve ending it passed, finally centering on the bundle of nerves in her clit. She shuddered against the assault.

"Okay, Sam, I'm going to take them off now."

He was still behind her, so he wouldn't be able to soothe her nipples with his mouth. She braced herself as he released the first clamp. Raw, clawing pain concentrated on her bruised nipple and she cried out, unable to stop herself. He massaged her breast, stroking the nipple, helping the pain dissipate. Then he removed the other one and the whole process began anew. All the while he remained against her, reassuring, calming.

"Are you all right? Do you want me to continue?"

"Of course, Sir."

Mike laughed and kissed her neck before he stepped back.

"Okay, girl. Here we go again!"

The flogger connected with her ass in a wake-up call, stinging far more than she expected. Mike knew how to wield that thing to its best advantage. Sam drifted a bit, losing touch with her surroundings, only conscious of the rhythmic strokes.

Until she felt the nasty bite of the dragontail. She hadn't even realized Mike had changed toys. But the sharp strike brought her out of her dreamlike state. Mike aimed mostly at her ass, stinging the same area over and over until she thought she wouldn't be able to stand any more. The delicious torment morphed into an electric tingling throughout her body, ratcheting up her desire to an agonizing peak. Again he seemed to know what she needed, stopping the whip so that he could press his body fully against her. His hands found her aching center and massaged gently. She leaned back, letting him know she needed more.

"Do you want to come, Sam? If you do, you have to ask for it."

"Please, Sir... May I come?"

"Not yet. I need you to suffer for me a little more."

Dammit! Her need escalated as he stepped back and resumed whipping her. He struck her shoulders, worked his way down to her ass, carefully avoiding her kidneys, then slowly retraced his route back up to her shoulders. Up and down, up and down, till she couldn't keep track of where he was anymore as she floated away on a cloud of sensation, free from all thought.

His voice penetrated her haze. "How are you doing, Sam?"

All she could manage was, "Mmmm."

"Sam, I'm taking you down."

"What?" she whispered as she slowly emerged from her stupor.

"Ssshhh. Just relax. I'm taking you down."

She settled back into oblivion. The next thing she knew she was curled up in Mike's lap with a blanket tucked around her. He smiled down at her.

"Hey, welcome back."

She tried to sit up, but gentle pressure kept her where she was. "You need to recuperate before you get up. Drink." He placed a water bottle with a straw in front of her and encouraged her to drink more even after she wanted to stop. When he seemed satisfied, he took it away and embraced her, stroking her as she closed her eyes and savored the feeling of safety and security.

Until she realized where she was and sat bolt upright.

"I'm good," she declared and tried to stand up.

"I don't think so," he countered, preventing her from moving. "You did so well, Sam, you didn't even get your reward yet." He repositioned her and had her straddle his legs. The blanket fell away. Fully exposed to his touch, her body came alive, her need front and center, demanding release. She had to feel his hands on her.

"Please," she moaned.

Blessedly, he didn't require her to say more. He stroked her breast with one hand and gently massaged her clit with the other. She tried to push upward to force him to apply more pressure, but he wouldn't allow it.

"Don't move. You follow my lead or we stop."

She sat back on his lap, feeling his arousal settle against her. She couldn't stop her involuntary chuckle after realizing he was as turned on as she was. Both of his hands stopped moving.

"Nooo…please…Sir!"

"First tell me what's so funny." He remained still.

"Not funny ha ha," she explained. "I'm just delighted you're as affected by me as I am by you."

"You can count on it," he said as his hands resumed their sublime work. "You have great power in your beauty, your responsiveness and especially in your submission."

"And you have magic hands, Sir." She sighed. Her muscles were tense, her breasts overstimulated and her clit was straining for release, but he didn't increase his pace. She was lost in a maelstrom of sensation, hungry for more. Finally—*God yes!*—he pinched both her nipple and her clit at the same time.

"Come now!" he demanded and she exploded, her whole body shaking uncontrollably. He held her tightly and she blissfully rode the intense orgasm till it leveled off, his firm hold centering her through the intense aftershocks that wracked her. Eventually she settled, still splayed against him but uncaring of how she looked.

Oh my God. I'll have more of that, please...Sir. But somehow she couldn't bring herself to share with him how much he affected her. He would have to be content with her submission. She wasn't giving him any more of herself. She had already given up too much.

Mike planted a sweet kiss on her head, then encouraged her to drink more water. She sucked the bottle dry in an attempt to revive herself. Now it was his turn to chuckle.

"What's so funny?" she asked as she turned to look at him. He smiled back at her, his grin broad.

"Not funny ha ha, just an appreciation of your gusto."

She wasn't sure if she liked the comment, but she wasn't about to argue with the man who had given her such heavenly gratification.

"Thank you, Sir... For everything."

"It was definitely my pleasure," Mike replied, stroking her cheek before he bent down and kissed her gently on the lips.

Uh-oh, too far. Sam didn't like gentle, particularly after a scene. It required that she open herself up in a way she wasn't comfortable with. *Time to redirect his attention.* She shimmied against his firm cock and turned to look at him.

"Isn't it your turn, Sir?"

Mike marveled at Sam's need to deflect affection. Not that he wasn't interested in some reciprocity. He just wanted to engage with her softer side for a moment, maybe open her up a bit more. But she wasn't having any of it. He'd have to let it go…for now.

"That's nice of you to ask," he replied. "You may proceed."

She was obviously more at ease with taking the lead as she slid off his lap and positioned herself on her knees in front of him. He rested against the sofa back and let her have her way.

Sam unbuckled his belt and drew down his zipper with a ravenous look on her face. Clearly this was her comfort zone, taking control and providing pleasure. He was sure she didn't even realize how submissive her actions were because he was allowing her to service him. He decided not to point that out. It could distract her from her mission, which she was conducting with relish.

A slight hesitation when she discovered the size of his cock didn't slow her down for long. She leaned forward and licked the pre-cum off his tip. Just as she reached up to grab him, he stopped her.

"Hands behind your back. Let's see if you can bring me off with just your mouth."

Her answering smirk told him she was confident she could accomplish the task without question. He was going to challenge her. If she didn't want tender, he'd give her rough. As soon as she opened her mouth he grabbed her hair and slid his cock deep, forcing her to gag.

He pulled back. "Too much?"

"No, Sir," she said through gritted teeth. "I can do it." She swiped at the tears now falling on her cheeks.

"I told you to keep your hands behind your back," he growled.

She quickly put her hands behind her and sat motionless for a moment. He wiped the tears away himself. She shuddered then took a few deep breaths. She looked so beautiful with the tracks of tears smudged across her cheeks, increasing her vulnerability. His cock felt like it would burst before he got it back into her mouth.

"I'm ready, Sir," she told him, her chin jutting forward in an apparent display of bravery.

"Are you sure? I'm not going to go easy on you," he warned.

"Yes, I'm sure, Sir."

Mike grabbed her hair and as soon as Sam opened her mouth he slid in, grazing her throat. This time she was prepared, having relaxed in anticipation of his assault. His whole body quivered as she closed her lips around him and massaged the underside of his cock with her tongue.

"Touché," he remarked. "Well done."

She met each of his subsequent thrusts with confidence, swallowing him, driving him insane. It didn't take long before he was ready to spill.

"Get ready. I'm going to come."

She barely nodded before he shot his cum down her throat. She took all he gave her, not losing a drop. Releasing him, she rested her head on his thigh as he collapsed, his hands still in her hair. He gently massaged her scalp.

"That was incredible," he told her. "Thank you."

"You're welcome, Sir."

He wasn't sure, but he thought he felt her smile against him. It made him smile as well. Then he made the stupid mistake. He patted her head.

Sam immediately stood up.

"It was a good scene, Sir. Thank you as well."

She turned, grabbed her clothes off the table and marched away, her luscious ass mocking him in retreat. Mike was astonished, but he damn well wasn't going to run after her.

Fuck!

He pulled himself together, then slowly collected his toys and wiped down the St. Andrew's cross. He needed to get his head on straight before he walked over to his friends. He wasn't going to let on that he'd been thrown off by Sam's hasty departure. When he returned to the bar area, he ordered a Scotch on the rocks and sipped it.

Ethan clapped a hand on his shoulder and leaned in. "Looked like a good scene," he remarked.

"Uh-huh. Better than I expected." Another sip and the Scotch began to calm him down.

"So when do you get to see her again?"

Ethan knew of his interest in Sam, but Mike didn't think now was the time to talk about it. He wanted to process what had happened and figure out his next move.

"Not sure. She left before we had a chance to discuss it."

Ethan huffed a laugh. "Yeah. I saw her quick exit. What the hell was that about?"

"Mixed signals, I think. It's hard to figure out what a sub needs when she's not sure herself."

"Tell me about it. It took a long time for me to get Rebecca to commit."

Mike shook his head. "But you knew why—that her son was an issue—so you could focus on that. I'm not sure what's holding Sam back."

Ethan shrugged. "Rebecca doesn't even know, and she's with her all the time. Sam's a good friend to everyone in the kitchen and doesn't hesitate to give her advice, but when it comes to opening up about herself, she's tight-lipped. Good luck, buddy."

Mike took another long sip of the Scotch. "Thanks. I'm gonna need it."

Chapter Two

Sam was the first one in the Catered Affairs kitchen on Tuesday morning. It was intentional. She wanted to be well into food prep by the time the others arrived so she could deflect the conversation away from Saturday night. She was still annoyed with herself for having scened with Mike. He was dangerous — too strong — and it had been far too easy to let go with him.

Not that she hadn't enjoyed it. She had to admit that it had been thrilling not being the one in charge. Mike hadn't let her get away with topping from the bottom. Being kept off balance had been exhilarating. She hadn't ever reached subspace quite like that before. Yes, she could drift off from pain, but there was a part of her that was always alert, making sure nothing went wrong. Being with Mike had been different, and she'd been able to truly let go. She knew deep down that he would keep her safe while she transcended the splendid pain he provided and floated off into her own world.

Not to mention the orgasm, that glorious ride to ecstasy. How he'd made that happen, she wasn't sure. It wasn't as though no one had ever massaged her clit before to bring her off. But his magic hands, combined with his take-no-prisoners dominance, had brought her to a level of pleasure she hadn't had in a long, long time. Not since the beginning of her relationship with Alex.

She closed her eyes and took a deep breath, erasing the thought of Alex from her brain. She didn't want to go there...ever again.

The arrival of Rebecca and Allegra helped her escape her reverie. A mixed blessing to be sure, because now she would have to fend off the questions she didn't want to answer.

"Hey, guys. I've got the potatoes and beans washed, so if you want to start on them, they're ready," she informed them.

"Allegra, why don't you take the potatoes and I'll let Mya do the beans when she arrives," Rebecca instructed as she donned her apron. "I'm going to start on the brownies. What do you have going, Sam?"

"I thought I'd get the salmon prepped." She pulled the gigantic fish out of the fridge and placed it on the stainless steel counter. Rebecca nodded her approval then started on her own task. Sam turned on the radio to her favorite oldies station and pumped up the volume. It looked like her tactic had worked.

Rebecca waited till Sam was halfway through removing the first side of the salmon before she walked over to the radio and turned it down. By this time Mya had also arrived and was tipping the beans.

"Okay, Sam. Your turn to tell the group about your Saturday night. We all have to confess when we come into work, soooo... How was the scene with Mike?"

So, maybe they'd seen through her plan. Sam waited till she got down to the bottom of the fish and had placed the fillet on a sheet pan before she turned to answer Rebecca. "It was good. Surprisingly good. I liked it. I think *he* liked it. Yeah, it was good."

She began to remove the salmon skin with serious concentration.

"Oh no no no no. You make us all give you the complete gory details," Rebecca responded. "We need a lot more than that."

Sam stalled until she was finished with her task. She threw the skin away and looked up at Rebecca.

"He was tough and rough, just the way I like it. I came hard, he came hard, and then it was over. I don't think I'll scene with him again. I scratched an itch I've had about him, and it's done. He's a strong-willed Dom and it was fun for an evening, but I don't think I want a repeat performance."

Before anyone could say a word, she set about removing the bone from the center of the fish. Rebecca finished measuring her flour, a look of consternation on her face. Then, as though she couldn't hold herself back any longer, she erupted. "I can't believe you! I watched the entire scene. Mike was amazing, and it looked like you were really into everything he was doing. Until you got up suddenly and walked away. What happened?"

"Nothing happened. The scene was over, it was time for me to leave. You know I'm not big on aftercare, and not everyone is made for each other like you and Ethan or Mya and Jake."

"I didn't think Jake was for me in the beginning either," Mya piped in. "It took a while to convince me. You should give Mike a chance."

Sam let out a sigh of frustration. "I'm going to say this one last time. Mike is not for me. He handles a dragontail the best of anyone I know, but it's not a good foundation for a relationship. So let's drop it, shall we? I can't stand talking about him anymore!"

Silence reigned in the kitchen. Sam turned up the radio again and began singing along to Bon Jovi's *Livin' on a Prayer* at the top of her lungs. Rebecca shouted at her above the din. "You win for now! But we're not done with it!"

Oh yes. We are.

* * * *

Mike sat in his car on the dark, deserted street, his eyes scanning every available way to approach the apartment building across from where he was parked. He was on a stakeout, watching to see if Andy Cooper—a petty thief who, out of his usual habit, had stolen a valuable necklace Mike was now trying to recover—would visit his last-known girlfriend. He had a tip that Andy had left a local bar and was probably coming in this direction. The job needed his attention but not enough that he couldn't also devise a plan to entice the elusive Sam into another scene.

He admitted to himself that he needed help. The idea of being submissive was so uncomfortable for Sam, he was sure she wouldn't acquiesce to scening with him again without a bit of subterfuge. The club was out. She would be much more careful about avoiding him so he couldn't nudge her into a scene like he had Saturday night. Rebecca was on his side. She was apparently invested in helping Sam recognize her submissive side. Maybe he could get Rebecca to help him figure out a plan.

His target approached the building. Mike was out of his car and on Andy before he reached the door. Not being a cop, he wasn't constrained by their rules of engagement. Despite Andy's larger size and bulk, Mike's military training and the element of surprise allowed him to push Andy up against the wall of the building and pull his arm behind his back before he realized Mike was there.

"What the hell you doin', man?" Andy demanded, trying to push Mike without success.

"We need to have a talk, Andy. You have something that doesn't belong to you, and I want it back."

Andy slumped against the wall.

"I don't know what you're talking about," he grumbled.

Mike pushed against him harder and applied a bit more pressure on the arm. Andy groaned.

"Yes. You do. And if you don't give it up, you're going to be very, very sorry." A bit more pressure on the arm.

"Hey, you're gonna to break it!" Andy shrieked.

"Yeah, I am, if you don't start talking," Mike threatened.

"You can't! I'll call the cops!"

"Go right ahead. I'll be glad to inform them of your whereabouts last night. I suspect you won't see the light of day for quite some time." More pressure.

Andy howled out an "Okay!" before Mike relaxed his grip. "If you let me go, I'll tell you what you wanna know."

"I'll let you go *after* you tell me what I want to know."

Andy didn't say a word. Mike waited out the weasel who didn't have the toughness to tread in the dangerous waters of high-value crime. Mike didn't know what had prompted Andy's foray into a world he was unfamiliar with and ill-equipped to handle, but Mike really didn't care. All he wanted was to retrieve the item.

Out of patience, Mike pushed against Andy again. "Now or never."

"Promise you won't turn me over to the police, and I'll tell you where it is."

"No bargains. Give it up or I won't be responsible for my actions." Another tug on the arm.

"Okay, okay! Just don't break it, please!" Mike let up a tiny bit. "It's in a locker at the train station. I needed a place to stash it till I could bring it to the fence."

"Give me the key."

"I will if you let me go. I can't get it with one hand behind my back." Andy's voice became a whine.

"Which pocket? If you don't move and let me get it, I'll let go of your arm," Mike informed him. "But don't try anything while I reach for it."

Andy nodded. "My shirt pocket."

Mike reached his other hand over Andy's shoulder and grabbed the key out of the pocket. He put it in his jeans.

"We're going to the station now to get the necklace. If it isn't there, you're going to wish you were dead before I'm done with you."

"Hey, you said you'd let me go if I gave you the key!" Andy protested.

"No," Mike clarified. "I said I'd let you go when you gave me the necklace. I don't have it in my hand, do I?"

He pulled Andy away from the building and led him with his arm still behind his back over to Mike's car and shoved him into the passenger seat. Mike then got in his face.

"I know where you live. I know where your girlfriend lives. I know where you drink and where you get your drugs. You will not try to escape or I will track you down again. You can count on it. And then I won't be so nice."

Andy nodded in understanding, and Mike got in his car and drove them to the train station. He grabbed Andy out of the car and took him over to the lockers. Sure enough, the necklace was sitting in a locker in a paper bag. After removing it, Mike turned to face Andy.

"I'm curious. Whatever possessed you to step up your game and steal something like this? It's not your area of expertise."

Andy raised his chin in defiance. "I got it, didn't I? They think they're so smart, but my buddy saw it when he was at the house fixing the heating system and knew it would be easy. And it was. They didn't even have an alarm system."

Mike laughed. "So you thought. Their security system got a lovely picture of you, clear as day. It was no problem tracking you down. Oh, and the cops are on their way."

"Hey, you said you'd let me go!"

Mike held up his hands. "I didn't say the cops wouldn't be there when I did."

Andy took off just as the police arrived at the station, but he didn't get far before they had him in cuffs. Mike's friend Cole, a cop he knew from when they were both in Special Forces, came over and shook his hand. Mike handed him the bag with the necklace.

"I owe you one," Cole said. "I knew you'd get him to give it up. If we picked him up, he'd cry lawyer before we even got into an interrogation room and we'd have a hard time recovering it. My sister will thank you in person."

"No problem. And the insurance finder's fee will make up for any trouble I had. It was easier than I expected."

Cole laughed and clapped him on the shoulder. "I had utmost faith in your abilities. Thanks again, buddy. Talk to you soon."

By the time Mike got in the car and drove away, the rest of the cops were gone. With the job accomplished, he was able to turn his complete attention to the lovely submissive he wanted to conquer. An idea formed. Tomorrow Rebecca was going to get a call.

* * * *

On Wednesday the kitchen was working like a finely tuned machine. They were almost a day ahead in prep for the anniversary party they were catering Friday night, and Rebecca had promised them all an early night if they were able to get the last of the hors d'oeuvres finished before five. The music was blaring and they were all singing along with Tina Turner in a rousing rendition of *Proud Mary*.

The trill of a phone broke through the din. Rebecca grabbed her phone and went into her office. Before long she came out with a huge smile on her face.

"What?" Sam asked, unable to curb her curiosity.

"I think we're going to have a play party this weekend. We don't have an event on Saturday night, so we can have some fun." Rebecca went back to shredding the duck for the quesadillas. "You're all invited, of course."

"I'd love to come, and I'm sure Jake will want to," Mya replied. "We haven't had a private party in a long time. I love the club, but it's nice to be a small group sometimes."

"Yeah, I can't wait," Allegra agreed. She carried her pot of polenta and spread it out over a sheet pan to cool and firm up for the base of their polenta squares. She looked over at Sam. "You're coming, right?"

Sam shrugged. "It depends on who else will be there. You all have people to be with. I don't want to be the odd man out."

"Don't worry," Rebecca assured her. "We're going to invite some singles as well, both Doms and subs."

Sam looked up from the filets of beef she was browning. "Oh no. I'm not going if *he's* there."

"Whoever do you mean?" Rebecca purred.

Despite the aromas wafting through the kitchen, Sam could smell the setup a mile away.

"Are you all in on this or is it just Rebecca who thinks she has a right to manipulate my life?"

Allegra's and Mya's blank looks told her all she needed to know.

"You know, Becs, it wasn't so long ago that you were beating Ethan off with a stick and you thought we were interfering too much in *your* life. What makes you think it's okay when you do it to me now?"

She angrily flipped the filets to brown on the other sides. Rebecca scooped the shredded duck into a large bowl and wiped her hands before she came over to stand by Sam.

"I'm just teasing you, Sam. But you're a big girl. You don't have to play with anyone you don't want to. There will be other men there and maybe one of them will suit you better than Mike. I don't want you to miss the party just because he's there, and I have to invite him. He's one of Ethan's friends."

She encircled Sam from behind and rested her head on Sam's shoulder. "You're my best friend, Sam. We started this business together. Don't be mad at me. I can't stand it."

Sam melted. She couldn't stay mad at Rebecca for long, particularly when it wasn't her fault Mike was a controlling son of a bitch. They were all part of a tight-knit group, and Sam knew Rebecca couldn't leave out a major player, especially someone who had helped save Mya's life and aided Ethan when his brother was in trouble. Mike was a decent man. She'd just have to give him a wide berth at the party.

Sam slowly turned and hugged Rebecca back. "I'm not mad at you, Becs. I'm mad at the situation. I'd rather not have to deal with Mike, but I'm not a baby. I know the word 'no' and how to use it. I'm sure the party will be fun."

Rebecca gave Sam a quick peck on the lips and returned to her duck. She poured in the spicy sauce and stirred until it coated all the pieces, then she began to lay out the tortillas so she could spread the mixture on them. A collective sigh of relief came from Allegra's and Mya's stations. *Crisis averted, for now.*

Chapter Three

Sam sat in her SUV for a few moments after arriving at Ethan and Rebecca's. Her nerves were getting the better of her and she needed to appear calm and collected when she walked through that door. *Dammit!* She felt like a teenager going to her first dance and she didn't like it.

Before she could pull herself together, there was a knock on her window. She looked up and her heart fell. Mike stood there, eyebrows raised in question, looking hot as hell in black slacks and a tight-fitting black T-shirt that outlined his trim but muscular body. Rather than get out, she turned the ignition and rolled the window down.

"Yes?" she asked, trying to sound unruffled.

Mike crouched so he could see her better, and the minute she connected with his steel-blue eyes, she involuntarily lowered her own. Fighting her instincts, she forced herself to look back up, only to find a self-satisfied grin on Mike's face.

Don't be smug. I'm not falling for your charm.

"Do you need help carrying anything in?" he asked.

Actually, she did, and if she blew him off he'd call her on it. He wasn't the type to let that go by. "Yeah. I have some food in the back."

Mike nodded, then stood and reached for the handle of the car door. Reluctantly, she rolled up the window, pulled out the key and stepped out when he opened the door. She ignored his outstretched hand. Despite the stilettos, she could exit a car quite nicely on her own.

Clearly unembarrassed by her snub, Mike dropped his hand, closed the car door and followed her to the back. After it was opened, he stepped closer. The heady combination of sandalwood soap mixed with his natural male scent was intoxicating. With her senses on high alert, she needed total concentration not to be absorbed by his presence.

"You can take the two large coolers and I'll bring in the rest," she instructed.

He reached in, stacked the two coolers, added two slightly smaller ones on top and pulled them out of the vehicle.

"Big man!" she teased in a breathy voice as he proceeded to bring them into the house. "I'm so impressed."

He didn't turn but his laugh was infectious. "Wait till you see what else I can do!" he taunted as he walked up the front steps.

"That's okay," she retorted. "I've seen enough."

She watched him maneuver through the front door without help, then she turned back and picked up the two small remaining trays. He was back to hold open the door for her as she approached.

"Thanks," she told him, "I can handle it."

"I'm sure you can. But there's nothing wrong with accepting help, is there?"

She rolled her eyes and entered the house. "Oh, thank you, Sir," she cooed as she pranced into the kitchen. As she laid the trays on the counter she looked back to see his reaction, but he was gone. *Good.* Maybe he'd leave her alone for the rest of the evening.

Brat! That woman needed someone to teach her a lesson in proper behavior! And maybe that someone would be him.

Mike shook off his annoyance as he walked into the living room. Ethan, Jake and Bob were engaged in a serious debate about who was going to win the World Series, as the playoffs were winding down. A good conversation to help keep his mind off the sultry sub in the kitchen, the one who was getting under his skin. He sat down and joined in the dismayed concern that the Yankees were going to go down in flames.

As the rest of the guests arrived, the chefs from Catered Affairs orchestrated the food while everyone else gathered in the cavernous living room. Ethan and Rebecca had purchased a new home together and the living area was perfect for entertaining. It had an open floor plan with a kitchen that flowed into the dining area, which led to a beautiful living room with a cathedral ceiling. Once the buffet table was laid out, Ethan stood up.

"Please, everyone, enjoy the glorious food our talented chefs have prepared. We're lucky to have such a great catering company among us, led by my lovely sub, Rebecca." After the applause died down, he continued. "The dungeon is downstairs in the finished basement, and whenever you're ready to play, feel free to go down there. I know we all know one another, but club rules still apply. If we hear 'red', we're going to pay attention. Otherwise, enjoy!"

Rebecca came over to give Ethan a kiss, then they led the way to the extravagant buffet. Chatter resumed as people served themselves and found their places around the long banquet table. Mike tracked Sam's movements, hoping to situate himself next to her, but she was like a moving target. She was the only one who seemed to find it necessary to replenish every item on the buffet. In order not to appear like a stalker, Mike sat down alone. Two couples soon flanked him, leaving no room for Sam.

She eventually seated herself at the opposite end of the table, engaging in a serious conversation with some guy he hadn't met before, but he knew she was acutely aware of his presence because she surreptitiously glanced in his direction more than once. *Game. On!* He could wait her out.

Not surprisingly, she didn't make it easy. But despite her best efforts, he was able to walk over to her as her dinner companion got up to get dessert.

"Sorry, someone else is sitting here, as you well know," she said in a huff the minute he sat down.

"Yes, I know, but it will take him a moment to choose among the many delicacies you've provided. In the meantime, we can negotiate our scene."

If her eyebrows had risen any higher, they would have left her face.

"No. Red. Stop. Whatever it is you'll respond to. Our last scene was nice, but it was a one-shot. Thanks, but no," she declared, shaking her head for emphasis.

"Sorry, but I noticed you looking at me even while you were talking to your dinner companion. I assumed you wanted me to come over after he left."

"Wow, you have balls, I'll give you that," she acknowledged. "But it doesn't mean I'm impressed by them."

"Maybe not. But you have to admit, if you weren't so afraid of submitting, you'd love to play with me again."

She got up and walked away without another word. *Okay, round one to Sam.* But it wasn't over. He knew Rebecca and Ethan had plans for the evening that would definitely work in his favor.

Arrogant. Just fucking arrogant! Yeah, it often went with being a Dom, but Mike was way off the charts. Did he really think he could goad her into playing again?

She began to pick up empty plates from the table in an effort to remove herself from the action, stacking them noisily on top of one another, trying to tamp down her frustration. She didn't want to play with Mike and she didn't want to play with James, her dinner companion, who seemed nice enough but would require way more effort than she wanted to expend to get him to play with her the way she wanted. Just as she was about to go into the kitchen with her empty plates, she was summoned into the living room, where the rest of the group had gathered. Reluctantly she placed the plates back on the table and stood by the entrance to the living room.

"We thought we'd play a game to warm things up before anyone went downstairs, if everyone is amenable," Ethan announced.

The general consensus was yes. Sam had a sinking feeling she was not going to like the way this played out.

"So here's how it goes. I have three baskets with cards in them. The first basket has the names of the Doms in the room, the second parts of the body, the third toys. Rebecca will pick a card from the Dom box. That person will pick a body part and a toy and then choose a sub to fulfill the task."

Uh-oh. This was definitely not going to work in her favor. A glance at Mike's grin and she knew she was in trouble.

"Wait," she cried out. "What's to stop a Dom from having a whole scene before anyone else has a try?"

"Good question, Sam. I was just about to say, each task has a time limit of two minutes."

Not great, but better than full rein. She took a seat and waited for the inevitable, feeling like a sacrificial lamb. Rebecca was going to get an earful the minute she could get her in private.

Rebecca reached into the basket and drew Jake's name. He in turn drew 'back of the knees' and 'a feather' from the other baskets.

Jake pointed to Mya, who rose to stand in front of him. He took the feather from the array of toys on the table and signaled for her to turn. He pulled her hands behind her back and held them with one of his own while he caressed her with the feather.

"Not much of a challenge," someone mumbled, but while the group watched Jake brush the feather lightly over the backs of Mya's knees and heard her purr with delight, they got very quiet. As she gyrated in pleasure, it became apparent that doing the task was only half the game. Watching it being performed was the other.

Once time was called a collective sigh emanated through the room.

Next up was Bob, who selected 'buttocks' and 'flogger' from the baskets. He walked over to a sub Sam had never seen before and helped her rise. He positioned her bent over with her hands supported on the back of a chair then raised her skirt to reveal a thong. Making sure he had room to swing, he started gently swatting her with the flogger, increasing the intensity until he got the ten-second warning, when he drew back and gave her such a strong swat, she cried out and rose up on her toes. Sam couldn't help but squirm while they went back to their places and another name was called.

"Mike."

Sam sat back and tried to make herself as small as possible in the vain hope that Mike wouldn't call on her, but she knew it was useless. This was the setup, and she would only look like a spoilsport if she declined to participate in the seemingly benign game.

Mike pointed to her before he even drew the cards. She rose slowly as he revealed her fate.

"Hmmm... 'nipples' and 'vibrator'. I think this will work," he mused as he selected a small U-shaped vibrator.

This was going to be rough. Her nipples were sensitive and he was going to make the most of it. She stood still as he approached and lowered the cups of her bustier.

"Lovely. Very lovely," he told her, then just stood there admiring her.

"You're holding up the show," she hissed. "Just get on with it."

Mike's sardonic grin mocked her, somewhat the way she had mocked him earlier.

"I get it," she conceded. "You've made your point. Can we just proceed?"

He didn't move. "I don't think you *do* get it," he enunciated quietly but very slowly.

Catching herself in an eye roll, Sam lowered her eyes. "May we proceed, Sir?"

"Yes, lovely girl, we may."

At Mike's nod, Rebecca started the timer. He placed the vibrator so it trapped a nipple between the two prongs of the vibe. He turned it on low and moved it up and down against her now-raised peak, forcing her to push her legs together to apply as much pressure as she could to assuage the tingling sensation at her core. Mike shook his head no and turned up the vibe's intensity as he insinuated his leg between her thighs and forced them open.

God, two minutes is endless. She was going to come before it was over and she didn't want to give Mike her satisfaction. She closed her eyes and tried to distract herself from the impending orgasm.

"Look at me," Mike insisted.

Her gaze was met with steel-blue eyes filled with such desire it was as though he had voiced it. Her body responded in kind.

Mike smiled, his expression diabolical as he lowered the intensity just as she was about to go over. *Bastard!* He pulled the vibrator off her nipple as soon as time was called, leaving her unfulfilled and shaking.

"Let's get you back to your seat." He put his arms around her, and as much as she wanted to resist, she let him lead her back to her chair. Instead of letting her sit on her own, Mike sat and pulled her onto his lap. Not wanting to cause a scene, she remained where she was. Mike planted a kiss on her head and she turned to give him a dirty look. Unfazed, he stroked her constantly while the next players completed their tasks. It got hotter and hotter in the room. By the time Ethan announced the game was over, Sam had been on the edge of orgasm so long she thought she'd disintegrate into a ball of goo. Her only consolation was that sitting on Mike's lap betrayed that he wasn't unaffected either. When he whispered his invitation to join him in the dungeon, Sam decided it was better to assuage her desire than win a battle.

Success! He took her hand and led her over to his toy bag, which he hoisted easily onto his shoulder. Then it was down to the dungeon, and miracle of miracles, she allowed him to guide her down the stairs so she wouldn't trip in her incredibly sexy but dangerously high heels.

He picked a station that had a hook suspended from the ceiling, wanting to keep her off balance. Not allowing her something to lean on, like a St. Andrew's cross or a spanking bench, would prevent her from hiding her face—and any telltale expressions—from him. It also allowed him full access to her body.

He turned to her. "Hard limits? Anything you don't want me to use?"

"No knives or drawing blood, no scat or golden showers, no violet wand. Otherwise I'm good."

"Okay, then. Lose everything but the stockings and shoes," he instructed before he turned to remove rope and a carabiner from his bag. She complied, and by the time she was done he had uncoiled the rope and stretched it. Beckoning her to stand under the hook, he placed the bight of the rope—the middle of the length curved on itself to create a loop—centered underneath her breasts, then brought the doubled-over rope around her torso and pulled it through the loop. As it tightened around her, she drew in a deep breath.

"Relax and breathe naturally," he directed. "I need the rope secure, and if you expand your chest it will be too loose and I'll have to start over. We don't want to delay our play with something like that, do we?"

"No, Sir," she answered, keeping her eyes lowered.

"You please me, Sam. I intend to reward you for your surrender to my wishes."

She smiled at him, and at that moment he had never seen her so beautiful. In her relaxed state—her furrowed brow and pursed lips gone—she looked radiant. He vowed to make sure she wanted to repeat the feeling.

He carefully wrapped her in a breast corset, ensuring that the doubled length of rope lay smoothly as it curled around her. He caressed her skin as he worked, enjoying how she leaned into his touch. As the rope bound her tighter, her breathing became shallower, her eyes dilating, her lips parting in a long sigh. She whimpered after he bound her hands behind her back.

"Color?" he asked.

"Very green, Sir."

He stroked her cheek, then trailed his hand down her torso till he could sweep his fingers through her wet core. She gasped in response to his exploration.

"Green, indeed," he confirmed with a small chuckle.

Keeping her close, he attached the carabiner to the hook and tied a second length of rope to the front of the corset. He wound it through the carabiner and pulled, which forced her up on her toes and raised her breasts higher. *Beautiful.* He slipped the rope through the corset and the carabiner multiple times then tied it off. When he was done, he stood back and admired his work.

She swayed slightly, but she was held securely by the rope, so there was no chance of her falling. Her nipples jutted out as though begging to be touched, and he indulged them for a while, rolling them between his fingers, slowly increasing the pressure till she moaned.

"How about a reward in the form of an orgasm?" he asked. "First of many I hope, as long as you behave."

"Yes. Please, Sir!" she cried, her desperation evident.

"Such nice manners," he praised. "You may come for me whenever you like."

He squeezed both her nipples hard then let go. He repeated the action over and over, sometimes pulling her forward while holding on to her tender buds, until she cried out and began to shake, unsteady on her feet. He continued to apply intense pressure, prolonging the orgasm while the rope kept her secure even as she swung unhindered. When she calmed, he embraced her and held her steady.

"Good?"

"Very good, Sir. Thank you for that."

"My pleasure. Nothing is more compelling than watching you come apart under my command."

She didn't answer, and he forced her chin upward so that she looked at him. He wanted her to see the pleasure, the desire, the satisfaction she aroused in him when she allowed her submission to envelop her. His power was impotent without her surrender. Even if it was just for a scene, nothing worked if she wasn't as committed as he was.

Wide-eyed, she perused his face, and it was obvious when she received his unspoken message. Her whole body softened and relaxed against him as she allowed him to support her. *Yes... Finally.*

He bent down and skimmed his lips against hers, and without any further inducement, she opened to let him in. He tightened his hold on her as he explored her mouth, her taste sweet on his tongue. She leaned against him and wrapped one leg around his waist, meeting his lust with a measure of her own.

By the time he pulled back from the ardent kiss, his cock was hard as a hammer and he wanted nothing more than to sink into her warm depths. It was only by calling upon his most ingrained sense of control that he didn't follow through. He needed to make this more than a mind-blowing fuck, to engage her in the spectacular dance of power dynamics so that she would need to come back for more whether she wanted to or not.

Gripping her hair, he pulled her head back and kissed her gently on her forehead, over her eyes, on her cheeks. When she tried to move toward him, he pulled tighter until she got the message — he was in charge and she was to stay where he placed her. He made his way to her neck, nipping at her flesh, creating little marks of possession. Her head fell back, further exposing her neck in a classic act of submission. In response he sucked hard at her tender skin, knowing he was creating a brand she would remember him by for days to come. Her answering cry revealed her capitulation.

He didn't let up. Holding her firmly with his hands at her sides, he kissed his way down her body, paying special attention to her now ultra-sensitized nipples.

"Your orgasms are free tonight. Whenever you want, just let go. It's my reward for your graceful submission," he told her as he laved her nipple.

A 'thank you' that evolved into a keening moan was her response as she came again.

Sam was lost in a sea of sensation. Held tightly by the embrace of Mike's rope and aroused by his insistent touch, she let go, surrendering herself into his care. He was demanding, but he generously gave back the more she allowed him control over her. Her resistance toward him faded into complete obedience.

He pulled over a chair and sat down in front of her, then raised her legs over his shoulders. She had just come and yet when he parted the lips of her pussy and blew on her clit, she clenched in anticipation. He sucked her clit into his mouth and tongued it firmly over and over until she crashed again, shaking uncontrollably while he palmed her ass cheeks to hold her fast and continued to lick her until she cried out, "Enough, please!" She could feel his broad grin against her tender flesh.

"I think you can take more. Enough is not a safeword, so if you really want me to stop, I need 'red'."

She remained silent.

"I thought so." He looked up at her with a twinkle in his eye, his amusement not as annoying as she would once have thought. He brought her to orgasm two more times before he gave her tortured clit some relief.

She closed her eyes and rested for a moment to prepare for what would come next. He was relentless, but how could she not like the attention he was lavishing on her? She wouldn't think about what she was giving up in return.

Mike brought her legs to the floor, stood and put the chair back where he'd found it. He came back and embraced her tightly, keeping her steady.

"Are you ready for some pain?" he whispered against her ear.

"Yes, Sir."

"Good."

He moved away, reached into his bag, and removed a blindfold, which he placed over her eyes. Her first instinct was to complain. Not being able to see what he was doing demanded the ultimate in trust. But she stopped herself as she realized she did trust him not to violate her hard limits or push her too far. She relaxed into the rope and waited.

He massaged her shoulders and stroked her along her arms. "Good girl," he praised. "I love when you give yourself over to me. Thank you." And she relished his approval, a warmth settling over her at the prospect of making him happy.

He released her and she heard him rifling through his toy bag. The next thing she knew, he was stroking her breasts. He lifted one and she felt a strong pinch above her nipple. Then another and another. Clothespins—forming a zipper. He circled her breast completely and ended with one directly on her nipple, forcing her to cry out.

"Give yourself over to it, lovely girl. Relax."

She almost did when he picked up her other breast and repeated the process. This time she was crying before he was finished.

"Are you all right?" he asked, gently wiping the tears that had escaped the blindfold. "Should I stop?"

"No, Sir." Even as the pain tormented her breasts, her body was aroused, ready for another orgasm.

"Spread your legs…wide," he commanded.

Uh-oh. She knew what was coming, but she opened to him despite her anticipation of the exquisite pain he was about to deliver.

He placed the clothespins along both sides of her labia. They were on a string, because she felt him tie it around the top of her thighs, which spread her labia apart, exposing her clit. She held her breath and steeled herself against the coup de grâce.

"Relax...relax, Sam. I won't do it until you relax for me."

Sam exhaled and willed her muscles to loosen. It took all her concentration not to tense in apprehension. Then it came. The ultimate pinch of pain on her clit, and she screamed as her whole body detonated in the inexorable orgasm. She swayed in the ropes, out of control, mindless in her ecstasy, climbing to increasing levels of pleasure. Through it all, Mike stroked her but didn't contain her movement. When she finally came down, she was wrung out.

"Ready to go again?"

"No! I can't!"

Mike nuzzled her neck. "We have to take them off, don't we?"

She leaned back against him. "Oh God, I don't know if I can stand it!"

"Of course you can. Just because you gave up control doesn't mean you've become weak. This is when you thrive, isn't it? When it gets tough, right, my lovely girl?"

Sam nodded despite herself. "Yes, Sir."

"Here we go," he warned, and the pins around her right breast flew off in a row, the final one on her nipple causing the most immediate pain. His mouth clamped down on the bruised nub, caressing it gently with his tongue, soothing away the pain from the blood rushing back in. When she sank against him, he pulled the zipper off her other breast and transferred his comfort to the newly tortured nipple. She whined in protest but pressed herself against him, silently begging for more. As soon as she settled, he prodded, "Ready?"

"Yes. Please just do it. I don't want to think about it."

"Where's the fun in that? The anticipation is almost as good as the act itself."

"For whom?" Sam cried out.

"Why, for both of us, right?"

"Do you have to make me admit I like it? Can't you just do it?"

He caressed her face, smoothing his thumbs over her cheeks in a placating gesture. "Admitting what you want is part of your submission, Sam. You have to own up to your desires. Only then will you get them fulfilled."

Sam didn't respond. Pain and pleasure roiled through her and she just wanted him to continue. But he waited her out till, in desperation, she exclaimed, "Yes, please, Sir, take them off!"

Mike took his time untying the strings around her legs before he pulled both lines off quickly, finally plucking off the clothespin tormenting her clit. As soon as his mouth began to assuage the excruciating pain, she once again shattered in an orgasm that wracked her whole body. Unable to stand, she had to trust his rope to hold her up during her trip to oblivion.

When she settled back into consciousness, Mike was holding her in a firm embrace, the blindfold gone.

"You are incredible, lovely girl. You let go with total abandon, holding nothing back, and it's a joy to watch."

He planted gentle kisses all over her face. "I'm going to take you down now."

He began to unravel the rope from the carabiner. When it became slack, he held her up as he removed the rest of it. He untied it from the rope corset and led her over to a large armchair, sitting and bringing her down onto his lap.

"May I have my hands back, Sir?"

He reached behind her to make sure they were warm, and after confirming they were, denied her request. "Our scene is not over and I'm not ready to release you. Unless you tell me you're in distress, you'll have to wait."

She didn't argue. She realized she felt totally comfortable bound in his rope—and his control. She closed her eyes and settled against him. He hugged her tightly and she indulged herself in his warmth and protection.

Mike realized Sam was sleeping when her breathing got deeper and steadier. He relaxed into the chair, enjoying the weight of the satisfied sub in his lap. He didn't even mind the discomfort from his own lack of release. The scene had been perfect. Sam had given herself to him without reservation, and she had confirmed everything he had believed about her—that she would be truly remarkable in her submission. She deserved to be treasured and nurtured…and pushed…until she realized her true self. He hoped she would continue to give him the opportunity to be the one who provided that for her.

She was such an enigma. On the one hand she was aloof and bratty. But when they played she submitted so beautifully, he couldn't figure out why she was so resistant to doing it. It was a mystery he would have to unravel in stages.

He kept checking her bonds to make sure she was still warm. He didn't want to release her until he was ready—he didn't trust that she wouldn't run off like she had the last time they played. It amazed him how she continued to sleep peacefully, unaffected by the noises of the other scenes going on around them. He had worn her out. *Good.*

Finally she stirred, opening her deep, chocolate brown eyes, which widened as she met his gaze.

"Hi. Did you have a good nap?"

She attempted to straighten up, but he held on to the rope so she couldn't rise. He caressed her arms while he spoke. "I want you to stay still for a moment so we can talk. It's called checking in after a scene. I'm sure you've heard of it, even though you didn't let me engage in it with you the last time."

"I'm not a big fan. I don't find it necessary either. I can take care of myself."

"I don't doubt that you can. But humor my inner Dom, who feels the need to make sure you're okay." He continued to caress her. "Did you enjoy the scene, Sam?"

It was quite remarkable the way her submission gave way to her inner brat right before his eyes. Her chin rose, her body stiffened, and though he couldn't see it, he was sure she rolled her eyes. "I would think it was obvious that I came more than once."

"I know you came many times. That's not what I asked. I asked if you enjoyed the scene, the way we interacted, the power exchange and the way you gave up your control to me. If all I wanted was to get you off,

I could have achieved that with a lot less effort. That wasn't what the scene was about, was it?"

He pulled her upright and turned her to face him, forcing her to meet his eyes. Once she looked at his stern expression, she lowered her eyes and blushed bright red.

"You don't want to admit it, but you got lost in the scene. You let go and allowed me to guide you, and it paid off, didn't it?"

He lifted her chin and was shocked by the tears that began to flow down her cheeks. "What is it, Sam? What is so wrong that you can't talk about it?"

Shaking her head, she leaned against his chest, shielding herself from his gaze. He cradled her in his arms and rocked her like he would a child. He didn't let go until she pushed back against him. Once she sat up, he begged her, "Talk to me, Sam. Please. I think we have something together. Call it chemistry, attraction, I don't know. We click and you know it. But we can't go on if we can't talk to each other. Communication is key. Please don't shut me out."

She took some time to collect herself. He was afraid she would totally close down, but eventually she spoke.

"You're right. You make me feel safe. I like ceding control to you when we scene. You take me to places I don't usually allow myself to go." She looked up at him, defiance written all over her face. "But I don't want to talk about it. I'm not ready to open myself up to anyone that completely. You can't have my innermost thoughts. Can't we just play without all the deep discussions? It's been good for me. If it isn't, I promise I'll let you know, all right?"

"We'll do it your way...for now. Let me get these ropes off you."

He began to uncoil the rope from her body, feeling as though he was releasing his tenuous hold on her in the process. Not at all what he wanted, but at least she'd left the door open for them to play again. It was a big concession on her part and he'd take it.

Once she was untied, she observed him carefully, her eyes grazing his body, stopping at his crotch.

"Don't you want me to take care of that for you, Sir?"

"I'd rather we take care of it together. I'm staying in one of the guest rooms. It would be nice if you would join me there."

"Okay," she responded with a slight shrug, her ambivalence rearing its ugly head once more.

"I'm not a kid unable to cope with a hard dick," he declared, putting his hands on her shoulders and gazing at her intently. "I want to make love to you, Sam. If you don't want that, we can wait for another time."

Again she shrugged. Fine. It was too soon. He would wait till she was ready. Until then, he could deal.

"Thank you for the lovely scene, Sam. I truly enjoyed it. I hope we can play again soon." This time he was the one who walked away, gathering his toys, giving her a quick peck on the forehead and leaving the dungeon. The surprised look on her face was almost worth it.

Sam hurriedly put on her clothes and went back upstairs. Mike was nowhere to be found, which was just as well as far as she was concerned. She went into the kitchen and began to clean up, allowing the routine of her chores help calm her down.

"In case you forgot, we hired people for the clean-up. They'll be here any minute," Rebecca said, standing at the entrance to the kitchen.

"I know. But I need to do something."

"Would that have something to do with the somber expression on Mike's face as he left?" Rebecca walked over to Sam and forced her to turn and look at her.

"I guess. Look, I did what you said. I surrendered to him in a scene, and it was really great. But I'm not into the 'make love' part of the evening." She exaggerated the air quotes.

"Too soon, huh?"

"If ever," Sam confirmed. "I'd play with him again. He's an excellent Top. But a relationship is out of the question. And so is 'making love'." She accompanied the air quotes with a look of irritation.

"I won't argue with you. So let's have a glass of wine and leave the clean-up to the crew we're paying."

Rebecca grabbed Sam's hand and led her into the living room. There were a few groups sitting and talking, so Rebecca steered them to a small alcove with a love seat. After pointing to Sam to sit, she went and got the wine.

"I feel like I've taken you from Ethan. I didn't want to do that," Sam apologized when Rebecca returned.

"Don't worry," her friend reassured her. "Ethan is a dungeon monitor since it's our house. When everyone goes home, it will be our turn."

Sam relaxed and took a sip of the wine. "Is your son coming back tomorrow from his father's house?"

"No, thank god. The guys need tomorrow to break down the dungeon equipment and put it back in storage. If Andrew was coming home tomorrow, we wouldn't have been able to have the party tonight."

Sam slipped out of her shoes and gathered her legs under her. "I don't know how you juggle it all.

Especially since Andrew doesn't spend as much time with his father as he used to."

"We've gotten very good at keeping our activities quiet. You'd be surprised how well a ball gag works." Rebecca followed Sam's lead and kicked off her shoes. "Ethan and Andrew are getting along. I never thought it would happen, but once we all moved in together, Andrew seems to have accepted the situation. And despite himself, he likes and trusts Ethan."

Sam stroked Rebecca's arm then clasped her hand. "I'm so glad it worked out after all you two went through together."

"It takes work, but if the man is worth it, the work is worth it. I don't regret a minute of it because we never would have gotten all this if we hadn't fought for it." She gave Sam a pointed look.

"I understand. But I'm not you, and we'll have to see what the future brings. Don't start looking for a wedding venue any time soon."

Rebecca laughed. "Deal, as long as you don't walk away from Mike without giving him a real chance."

Sam rolled her eyes, but Rebecca didn't let her off the hook. Ultimately she conceded. "Fine, I'll try."

Rebecca gave her a big hug. "That's my girl. I think you'll be glad you did."

Well, Sam thought, *only time will tell.*

Chapter Four

Mike stepped into Eagan's Pub and breathed a sigh of relief. Sitting and having a few drinks with his friends would help take his mind off Sam. Jake waved at him from the back booth and Mike stopped off at the bar to order a beer before he made his way over to where they were seated.

"You're just in time. We haven't ordered food yet," Ethan informed him.

"That's good. I'm starving. I haven't had anything since breakfast."

Once the waitress brought over his beer, they all ordered. Mike sat back and took a sip of the refreshing brew.

"So what happened to you last Saturday night?" Bob asked. "You seemed to have a good scene with Sam, then you left early."

"That woman has such a big wall erected around her it's hard to get through. We did have a great scene, and then she hunkered back down behind her defenses. I'm not sure how to get her to open up to me."

"If she's that closed-up, it has to be because something significant happened to her. It will take time to earn her trust," Bob counseled.

"Don't you think I get that? It's just so frustrating because when she does let go, it's incredible. And she seems to have just the right masochistic streak to suit me." Mike expelled a sigh of exasperation.

Ethan smiled at him. "I get it. I have that with Rebecca. It's nice when your sub responds to your sadistic impulses the way you want her to."

Bob gave Ethan a shushing sign, and everyone looked up to see the waitress approach with their food. They dutifully waited until all the plates were placed on the table and she walked away before they resumed the conversation.

"Well, I don't know how much time I'll have to pursue her. I have a case that's going to consume a lot of my time. I may even have to disappear for a while."

"What are you getting involved in? I don't have to worry about bailing you out of jail, do I?" Bob asked.

"I hope not. This is actually a personal matter. The daughter of an old Special Forces buddy has gotten involved with a guy who's in the Pagan motorcycle club. They're involved in drugs and organized crime here in Jersey. He wants me to help extricate her from the situation, but if I just remove her, I'm sure she'll go running back to the boyfriend. And she's not underage, so my friend can't force her to do anything. First I have to find her. Then I'm going to keep an eye on them and, if I can, try to convince her to leave before she gets hurt, which seems inevitable if she sticks with him."

"Good luck with that one," Ethan interjected. "I know from personal experience how difficult that can be. I couldn't get Zach to leave Gina, even though she was a leech. We got lucky when *she* left him. And then, as you know, things got even worse."

"I have to at least try. If it hadn't been for Derek, I'd be dead instead of just sporting a lovely scar." Mike touched the angry line of red that traversed his neck. The memory of Derek lifting him up after he'd been knifed during a guerrilla attack in Afghanistan and carrying him to safety would be seared in his mind for all time. Anything the man wanted in return, he would do.

"Maybe leaving Sam alone for a while will do some good," Jake suggested. "She might realize she misses you."

"Not likely, but I hope to see her a few times before I go undercover. I need to get the lay of the land before I try to insert myself into this gang's territory."

"I know I don't have to tell you to be careful, but be careful," Bob cautioned. "I'm getting used to having you at my beck and call when I need an investigator."

Mike smirked at him. "Believe me, I'm going to try not to fuck it up." He had some unfinished business with a bratty sub.

* * * *

Sam was just about to call it a night when her phone rang. It wasn't a number she recognized, so she ignored it, silencing the sound as she went into her bathroom to brush her teeth. A few minutes later the phone dinged, signaling a text. She finished washing and moisturizing her face before she returned to her bedroom and climbed into bed. The insistent blinking light on her phone compelled her to look at the text. It came from the unknown number that had previously called.

Tried to call to make a date. When you have a chance, give me a call. Mike

A date. One more step into a relationship. This wasn't just play, this was talking and sharing and confiding — all things she avoided like the plague. *Too intimate.*

Don't really do dates. Could meet you at the club sometime.

Mike's response was immediate.

Can I call you now?

Sam sighed, conflicted as to whether she wanted to talk to him. She was tired and not quite sharp enough to fend off any of his attempts to push her where she didn't want to go. But she did want to play with him again. The orgasms he gave her were mind-blowing, and she felt safe under his control — at least while they played. She gave in.

Sure.

The phone rang immediately.
"Hi," she answered.
"Hi. Hope it's not too late. I figured you work later when the weekend gets closer."
"You're right. But I can't talk too much because we have long days ahead of us. I'm already in bed." She

sank down onto her pillow, a reminder to herself to keep it short.

"And what are you wearing in bed?"

"A long flannel nightgown with long sleeves and a high neck." It wasn't true. She always slept naked. It was the one vestige from her relationship with Alex that she couldn't let go. Sliding into a cool bed at night, allowing herself the tactile enjoyment of being caressed by her silk sheets, was a pleasure she wasn't willing to give up despite the fact that it was Alex who had made her sleep naked for the first time. She'd decided she didn't have to give up her sensuality when she gave up her submission.

Mike's hearty laugh brought her swiftly back to the present. "I don't believe you. Lying to your Dom is cause for punishment." His commanding tone caused her to squirm, but she wasn't about to give in to him.

"First of all, you're not *my* Dom. And second, it's your word against mine."

Again Mike laughed. "Okay. You're right. I can't prove it unless I come over there."

"Not going to happen," she interjected before he took that idea any further.

"I'll put the punishment aside for the moment. Would you entertain the idea of some pleasure instead?"

Sam caressed her breasts in response. She was unable to prevent a little whimper before she realized what was happening.

"You seem to like the idea," Mike commented matter-of-factly. "Why don't you remove the granny gown?"

Sam hesitated for a moment, dangling on the precipice between fear and desire.

"You have total control here, Sam. You don't have to do anything you don't want to. I can't even touch you or push you past your comfort zone from afar. It's all in your hands, so to speak."

His soothing voice lulled her into agreement.

"Okay." She rustled her hands along the covers so he would think she was removing the nightgown. "It's off," she informed him.

"Good girl. But remember, just because I'm not there doesn't mean you don't use your manners."

"Yes, Sir," she answered without thinking.

"Do you have a vibrator close by?"

"Of course."

"Of course, Sir," he corrected, a hint of suppressed laughter evident in his voice.

Sam was grateful he couldn't see her eye roll as she responded properly, trying to keep the sarcasm from her tone. "Of course, Sir."

"Let's see if you can adjust your attitude while you reach for your vibrator, otherwise we'll stop right now."

Damn, he was relentless in demanding she submit, despite his reassurance that she was in control. Of course, he couldn't touch her now, but his command was unmistakable even when he only had his voice available. She decided she wanted to see where he would take her more than she wanted to defy him.

"I've got it, Sir," she told him, due deference in her tone, after she pulled the vibrator from the drawer.

"So what kind of playful device do you have?"

"It's a Hitachi."

"Why am I not surprised? I guess I would expect nothing less from someone as intense as you are."

"Thank you, Sir?" she responded, not sure if he was complimenting her or not.

"I love that about you, Sam. Don't think for a second that intense is a bad thing."

She relaxed into the sheets again, glad that he appreciated her level of desire. Alex had criticized her for the passion she revealed when she let go. He had wanted docile. She would never be docile. And he had made her feel guilty about it all the time they were together. Once again, Mike's soothing voice brought her back to the present.

"Place the Hitachi next to you and put your phone on speaker. Then I want you to stroke your nipples with the open palms of your hands. For this to work, I need you to acknowledge my instructions, and you have to be expressive as to what's happening to you. I want to hear your moans of pleasure, your whimpers of frustration."

"Frustration, Sir? I thought you said this was about pleasure."

"Pleasure comes in many forms, Sam. Waiting on the edge of fulfillment can be pleasure, am I right?"

He had a point, one she didn't want to concede. "Sam, I asked you a question. I expect an answer."

She sighed but answered "I guess you're right, Sir."

"Now that we have that settled, let's get started. Lightly brush your nipples as I instructed."

"Yes, Sir."

She pushed her blanket down, revealing her nipples. Brushing them back and forth with her palms eventually set her on edge. She needed to squeeze them, hard, and she was just about to when his voice came back over the line.

"Nothing more than lightly brushing them. Am I clear?"

"So we're going straight to frustration, Sir?"

Once again his hearty laugh boomed. "Brushing your nipples doesn't feel good?"

"Yes, it does. But I want more."

"And who gets to determine how much you get?"

"You do, Sir. But I don't have to like it."

This time his laughter was subdued, more like a chuckle. "I thought we just established brushing your nipples feels good. So relax and enjoy the feeling."

"Fine, Sir."

She took a deep centering breath, closed her eyes and resumed her task. Tiny ripples of pleasure traversed her body, all concentrating on the now tight bundle of nerves between her thighs. She was sure he could hear her labored breathing and the uncontrolled movement of her legs underneath her covers.

"That's it... Keep going... Enjoy," he encouraged.

"Please, Sir," she gasped, wanting more, needing more.

"No, Sam. I know your nipples are extremely sensitive. Just keep brushing and we'll see what happens. But you must calm down and stop fighting me. Breathe through your nose, relax your muscles, but don't stop stroking those nipples."

She followed his orders, opening herself up to enjoying what he was giving her. As he encouraged her to relax and surrender, she drifted off into the lovely sensations she was experiencing. The pressure in her clit intensified as well, and soon her whole body began to tremble. Suddenly she came, flying off into unbridled bliss. Mike's "Yes, let go!" pushed her further, prolonging the orgasm, till she came back down to earth.

It took her a moment to realize she hadn't asked for permission for the delightful orgasm.

"Sorry, Sir," she said, hoping her voice exhibited proper contrition.

"You went exactly where I wanted you to go. I'm not mad. I know it took you by surprise. I hope you realize now that gentle can be just as effective as intense. And you can enjoy both."

"I'll say. I can't believe I came from that little bit of stimulation."

"It didn't happen just from stimulation. You let go and gave over to my control, and in the process you found gratification—as did I, I might add. I loved hearing your moans of ecstasy."

She remembered her manners. "Thank you, Sir. I did enjoy it."

"We work well together. I'd like to have the opportunity to explore with you more. Is it so bad that I'd like to have dinner with you beforehand?"

Clever man, bringing me back to the idea of a date in such an innocuous manner. "I guess not."

"I realize you're busy with work the rest of this week. How does Monday night sound?"

"Monday will be fine."

"Good. I'll pick you up at 6:30. Wear something silky for me. And no panties. Good night, sweet girl. Get a good rest."

And just like that he was gone, leaving her slightly amused at his manipulation. He'd gotten the date he wanted and given her an orgasm to assuage her discomfort over it.

She put her phone on the nightstand and had turned to curl up on her side when she spied the Hitachi. He had set her up to believe he was going to have her use the device to bring herself off. Then he'd brought her along with gentle persuasion till she'd exploded. It had been the perfect mindfuck. Apparently he was an expert at it.

After replacing the Hitachi in her bedside table, she burrowed under the covers. Her own laughter at the situation overcame her much like the orgasm had. He certainly kept her on her toes. If she wasn't careful, he would insinuate himself into her life in such a way it would be difficult to extricate him.

Chapter Five

It had been a rough weekend. If anything could go wrong, it did. Incorrect deliveries, a broken-down van, a venue that had promised equipment they needed that wasn't there when they arrived. Sam's head had been spinning helping Rebecca figure out how to solve the endless problems that presented themselves. And they'd had to feed two hundred and fifty people at an elaborate wedding on Saturday and fifty people for Sunday brunch.

As usual, it had all worked out. They were good at what they did. But Sam was totally drained and tempted to cancel her date with Mike. Only the memory of the phone call she'd had with him days before kept her from doing so.

She knew it was Rebecca when her phone rang around five o'clock in the afternoon.

"Don't you have to take your son somewhere or pick him up?" she challenged when she answered.

Rebecca was unfazed. "So what are you going to wear?"

Sam knew she wouldn't get off the phone until Rebecca was satisfied she'd be dressed appropriately for her date.

"I figured I'd wear the black lace. It's the perfect combination of sweet and sexy."

"Didn't he tell you to wear something silky?" Rebecca countered. "I think you should wear the red silk. It's the perfect combination of sultry and slutty."

Sam couldn't help but laugh. "That's a club dress. I don't usually wear it out among the vanillas."

"It's not that bad. And you want to knock him off his pins. That dress will do it."

It was a good dress, hugging her in all the right places, with a slit up the front that promised great treasure underneath. With her red stilettos, it was a knockout. She usually got whoever and whatever she wanted when she wore it. Maybe Rebecca had a point.

"All right," she conceded.

"And wear your hair down," Rebecca instructed. "The red in your hair really shines when you wear that red dress."

"Anything else? Or can I be trusted to pick a bra and do my makeup on my own?"

"Actually I think you should wear that bra with the cutout nipples you bought in Lingerie Heaven."

"Absolutely not! With the silk of the dress I'm not walking around with my nipples pushing up against the fabric. That's too far."

"Just trying to help."

Sam laughed. "I appreciate it. And I promise to wear the red dress. But I'll figure out the rest. Go make dinner for your family or something."

"I want you to relax and have a good time. You deserve it, Sam."

A sudden rush of tears took Sam by surprise. Quickly wiping them away, she tried to be calm when she responded to Rebecca's caring words. "I promise to be open to whatever happens this evening. I love you for looking out for me, but I'll be fine."

"I love you too, sweetie." The sound of a kiss came over the line just before Rebecca hung up.

Sam collected herself and went in to take a shower. As the hot water rained down on her, she reflected on how lucky she was to have a good friend like Rebecca. Rebecca's offer to join her business had come at the right time. She had just gotten up the courage to leave Alex, and the start of a new business had been the perfect distraction from her depression. She didn't think Rebecca had realized she was in such bad shape at the time. Although they had been friends in culinary school, and they had really gotten close working together, Sam had never revealed how bad her relationship with Alex had been.

She grabbed her loofah and started to wash, keeping herself from going any further into her thoughts of Alex. That was best left to distant memory. By the time she was dressed and ready for her date, Sam realized she was actually excited. When her doorbell rang, she had to force herself to walk slowly to open the door. And to not lick her lips when she saw Mike.

He was dressed in a light-blue button-down shirt that brought out the blue in his eyes. Black slacks gently hugged his trim hips. And his admiring smile reflected his appreciation of her appearance.

"Wow. Just wow," he murmured, regarding her from head to toe with the look of the wolf seeing Little Red Riding Hood for the first time.

An unfamiliar feeling of shyness overtook her in the face of his unabashed admiration. "I'm glad it meets your approval."

"It certainly does. I'm a very lucky man." She stepped aside as he came into her house. "Are you ready? I think I picked a place for dinner that will meet with your approval."

"Yes. Just let me get my purse and jacket."

"Wait. Before you do that, I want you to show me that you followed my instructions to not wear panties."

"Sure, Sir." If he wanted a show, she'd give it to him. She turned, raised her dress and bent forward, exposing her red garter belt and all her assets. His hiss of approval was her reward.

"Very nice, Sam. Very, very nice." His hand grazed her ass cheek before he pushed her dress back down. "That vision will stick with me all through dinner."

She turned, flashing him a saucy smile before she went to collect her things from her bedroom. On her return, he enveloped her in a bear hug and kissed her deeply. She melted into his arms, softening against his hard body, attuned to his demand. She was disappointed when he broke off the kiss.

"If we don't leave now, we'll never make it to dinner." He grabbed her hand and preceded her out, standing impossibly close while she locked up, then leading her to his car, where he opened the door and handed her in.

They were quiet on the ride to the restaurant, but it was a companionable silence. He placed her hand on his thigh and held it the whole time. By the time they got there she was relaxed and looking forward to dinner.

The restaurant was lovely, located by the Hudson River and overlooking the New York City skyline. It wasn't warm enough to sit outside, but Mike had reserved a table by the window where the view was unobstructed. She had been a bit surprised when they'd driven up because she hadn't expected him to pick such an elegant place. She realized she had assumed that his profession and his implacable strength and confidence made him rough around the edges, but if she really thought about it, his attention to her had always displayed a deep understanding of her needs and desires. He was a complex man, with more sides than she gave him credit for.

Mike interrupted her thoughts. "Would you like a cocktail or wine with dinner? Unless you'd like both, in which case we can postpone our play for another time."

"Wine with dinner is fine. I don't really drink that much anyway," she responded, then hesitated. She wasn't sure she wanted the answer to her next question, but she asked it anyway. "Would you really want to only have dinner and not play?"

Mike sat back and regarded her seriously, his brow furrowed. "Is it so difficult for you to have a nice dinner and talk and get to know each other without it leading to a scene? I like you, Sam. I would enjoy spending time in conversation as much as engaging in play. Why are you so resistant to opening up to someone?"

"It hasn't worked well for me in the past," she told him, the tension now pressing in on her neck muscles, making her uncomfortable. "And no, I don't want to go into details."

Mike watched Sam transform before his eyes. Her eyes went dead and her whole body curled in on itself, making her seem so vulnerable. He reached across the table and took her hand in his, gently massaging with his thumb. It didn't appear to do much good.

"Hey, I'm not trying to pry into your deepest, darkest secrets. Those kinds of revelations require way more trust than I think we've built up to this point. I do, however, want to know more about you. Do you like the outdoors? What movies and books are your favorites? Things like that. Can't we start from there?"

Sam seemed to relax a little. "Yes, we can. But you asked a question that went way beyond that, which is a hard limit for me right now."

"You're right. I won't make that mistake again." He squeezed her hand then let go. "Why don't we look at the menu, and I'll learn about the kinds of food you like to eat."

She smiled at him, her eyes lighting up again, and he expelled a breath he hadn't even realized he was holding. Being around Sam was like walking a tightrope. He'd have to be very careful, but deep inside he knew it would be worth the effort…and patience.

She spent a great deal of time deciding what to eat. He was glad to have chosen a place that appealed to her sophisticated palate. He tended more to simpler fare and ethnic cuisine, but exploring this side of her was proving to be even more fun than he anticipated. As he listened to her discuss the merits of each menu item, he appreciated her enthusiasm for picking the right combination of dishes to create a perfect dining experience. Of course, they'd have to share, since she couldn't narrow her selections down to only one dish per course. He was prepared to order more than two of each to make her happy, but she wouldn't let him. She then chose a crisp, full-bodied Pouilly-Fuissé to go with the meal. By the time they were done ordering, her whole demeanor had changed.

"This is such a wonderful place. How did you find it?" she asked.

"I did an Internet search on best restaurants in New Jersey. I wanted to find a place that would allow you to experience the kind of food you create without having to cook it yourself."

She rewarded his effort with an approving smile. "I don't often get to stretch my culinary skills quite like this. Most clients usually want filet of beef because they think it's the most impressive. We have a hard time making them realize that anything can be made exceptional if you're creative with it. People are afraid to try new foods, particularly when they host a party, even when we provide a tasting of things they could have. I get it, but it's not as much fun as working in a restaurant like this. Sometimes I really miss it."

"Why did you leave?"

"Rebecca offered me an opportunity I couldn't refuse. If I'm honest with myself, by the time she presented me with the chance to become her partner, I was ready to work for myself."

"Well, you can cook for me anytime," he offered. "I'm open to anything."

"I bet you are," she answered with a grin.

At that moment the waiter arrived with wine. Mike told him to have Sam taste it. Not long after, their first course came. Sam surveyed their offerings and took in a deep breath, then commented, "Perfect. Lots of garlic in the mussels, and the octopus looks expertly charred."

He cut off a piece of the octopus and the accompanying pork belly, swirled it in the leek puree and offered it to her. She leaned forward, slowly removed the tidbit from the fork and moaned softly in pleasure. "Mmm, yes, expertly charred, sweet and salty, very rich. Try some."

It was as good as she said it was. She fed him a taste of the mussels with chorizo cooked in a fragrant tomato sauce, and he liked it as much as she did. They took turns eating and feeding each other in an intimate exchange of pleasure. Every once in a while, she would groan in delight and his cock would respond in kind. As much as he was enjoying himself, it was going to be difficult to maintain his composure throughout the meal.

By the time the second course arrived, he was regretting the choice of table. As nice as it was to look out the window, he would have preferred sitting next to her in one of the booths in the back. He needed to get his hands on her. Once the waiter left, he looked across the table to see her broad smile, her eyes twinkling with mischief.

"Great foreplay, right?" she asked as she offered him a piece of butter-soaked lobster. Putting it into his mouth, savoring the sweet morsel, he then smiled in agreement.

"Absolutely. I can't wait to taste you as well."

She blushed. It surprised him whenever she did it, because he'd believed she was too self-confident to blush. Was she finally tapping into her submissive nature, trusting him with her vulnerability? If so, they'd made more progress than he'd expected.

Throughout the rest of the meal she teased him either by feeding him or exaggerating her own enjoyment to the point that he wasn't sure he could stand up without embarrassing himself.

"You know you'll pay for your behavior when I get you home, don't you?" he warned her in a stern tone.

She batted her long, dark eyelashes at him and replied, "I don't know what you mean, Sir."

His raised eyebrow was greeted with a joyful laugh, one he couldn't help but join in. When the waiter came to ask if they wanted an after-dinner drink, he declined without even asking Sam. He needed to get her out of there.

An unexpected rain had begun while they were eating, so Mike had Sam wait inside the door while he got the car. By the time he returned, he was dismayed to see Sam fleeing the restaurant, a distraught look on her face, with a well-dressed man following her, apparently trying to talk to her. The man grabbed her by the arm and before Mike could get to her, Sam had hauled back and punched him in the face, knocking him to the ground. Mike rushed over and pulled the son of a bitch to his feet, ready to have a go at him himself, when Sam stopped him.

"Leave the bastard alone," she implored, her hand on his shoulder. "I probably shouldn't have hit him myself."

"No one puts their hands on my girl," Mike growled. "What the *fuck* were you doing?" Mike demanded, getting into the bastard's face.

"I was trying to say hello to an old friend," he replied, but his sheepish expression told Mike it was more than that.

"Let him go, Mike, please! Let's just get out of here," Sam begged, her voice shaky.

Still holding the man's jacket, Mike warned, "If I ever see you near her again, I will rearrange your face far more than she did. Am I clear?"

The man nodded furiously and Mike pushed the creep away. Mike turned to Sam, who looked so forlorn, her wet hair plastered to her head, the skirt of her silk dress clinging to her legs, tracks of tears washing her makeup down her face. He needed to get her out of there more than he needed to teach this guy a lesson.

"Come," he said, putting his arm around her and leading her to the car. By the time he got in himself, the asshole was gone. Sam was leaning against the door, establishing as much distance between them as she could. He reached out to stroke her arm but she flinched from his touch. *Fuck!* He'd like to kill that son of a bitch who'd turned the flirty, happy woman he'd had dinner with into the bedraggled, closed-up creature she was now.

He drove toward her house, trying to figure out what to do. He didn't want to drop her off and leave her alone, although he was sure that would be her preference. Yet he knew she wasn't ready to open up to him and reveal why she was so upset with the prick from the restaurant. He had to convince her to let him into her house, if not her confidence.

When they pulled up to her place, she grabbed the door handle.

"No, Sam. Wait for me to get you out," he instructed, his voice quiet but firm. Miraculously she dropped her hand and slumped back against the door. He quickly got out and rounded the car before she changed her mind. She took his proffered hand but didn't look at him as she emerged. He didn't let go as they walked up the stairs to her front door. She fished out her keys and, once the door was open, she turned to him.

"Thanks for a lovely dinner, but I need to be alone now."

"I disagree. You don't have to talk about it, but I don't want you to be by yourself. You're distraught, and I'd like to take care of you."

She didn't refuse him immediately and he stood, waiting her out, while she thought about his offer. Eventually, she shrugged and walked inside without closing the door behind her. An ambivalent invitation, but he took it.

Sam was numb. She heard Mike close the front door, but she didn't look back. She walked down the hall with the sole intention of crawling into bed, but before she was able to, Mike embraced her from behind.

"You have to take off those wet clothes," he told her. "Let me help you."

She had no energy to fight him. She had expended it all on fighting off Alex, not just physically but emotionally. She allowed Mike to peel the wet clothes from her body till she was naked, but before she could continue her journey to the blessed oblivion of her bed, he stopped her.

"I need to dry you off. Don't move." He rushed into the bathroom and emerged with a towel. She stood dutifully still as he rubbed her down then squeezed the moisture from her hair.

"Now you can get into bed."

He pulled back the covers, and once she got in, he tucked her in securely. She was mildly surprised when he didn't join her, but she didn't care one way or the other. All she wanted was to sleep…and to forget.

Unfortunately, sleep didn't come. Alex's voice kept playing in her head and she couldn't shut him out. *'Does he know you're a controlling bitch, that you'll never really submit?'* The question swirled on an endless loop, tormenting her, taunting her. When the long, desperate scream finally escaped from her gut, Mike was there, holding her, rocking her, soothing her with a quiet, "Ssshhh, I'm right here, baby. Relax…relax."

But she couldn't relax, and as she rested against Mike's chest, fury replaced her despair. How had she let Alex get under her skin with just one stupid comment? She had resurrected herself after leaving him, and with one chance meeting she had allowed him to push her over the edge right back to the days before she'd left him. *What's wrong with me?* She wasn't that weakling anymore, and she couldn't allow herself to wallow in the feeling of inadequacy he provoked in her.

She extricated herself from Mike's embrace and got out of bed. "I'm fine now. All I need is a shower. You can go. I'm really fine."

He regarded her as though she had grown two heads. "One, I don't think so. And two, I'm not leaving till I'm sure you're okay."

She wasn't going to argue with him. She went into her bathroom and turned on the shower. Once under the hot spray, she closed her eyes and let the water cascade down her body, wrapping her in its comforting heat. Her muscles relaxed and she forced the fury to dissipate as well. She didn't want any of those negative emotions dominating her anymore. She had regained control of her life and she wasn't going to allow anyone back into the position of determining how she was going to feel again.

She washed up and exited the shower to find Mike standing there with a towel open for her to step into. She plucked it from his hands and wrapped it around herself. He just watched as she dried off. Once she'd put the towel on the rack, she exited the bathroom and went to put on a robe.

"I'd prefer it if you stayed naked," he told her.

She rounded on him, her rage returning. "I don't really care what *you* want right now. I need to take care of myself! It's the only way it works for me."

He remained leaning on the doorjamb of the bathroom with his arms crossed, giving her the physical distance she needed. But it was clear he wasn't going to back down from her anger.

"I understand you've been taking care of yourself," he said quietly and calmly. "And you do a damned good job of it. I can't believe you decked that guy." His lips began to curl into a smile he seemed to think better of, but his eyes still sparkled as he schooled himself into a straight face. "All I'm hoping for is that you'll talk to me about what happened. Who was he?"

Sam expelled a long sigh of exasperation as she sat down on the bed, her robe still in her hands. Did she really want to go into all this with Mike? She fell back on the bed, her right hand over her forehead, and closed her eyes.

Could she confess to him what an idiot she'd been? Could she admit to anyone in her current circle of friends that she had allowed a man to take over her existence and isolate her from friends and family while he'd torn down her self-confidence and sense of dignity? Tears welled up, and she wasn't sure if they were from anger or shame.

"Fuuuuuuuck!"

She sat up to find Mike standing by her bedside. He must be a good detective—she hadn't heard him approach.

"Let it out. Shout at me if you need to, but tell me what happened. If you don't it'll eat you up inside."

He reached out and took her hand, and suddenly all the fight left her.

"He's my former Dom," she admitted. "It wasn't a good relationship, and it ended with me getting up the courage to walk out on him. He came up to me while I was waiting for you and apparently he's still holding a grudge, because he said some nasty things. I'm never going to take that kind of shit from him again."

"I'm proud of you for standing up to him. But it's still eating you up inside and you need a way to let it go. I can help you with that."

Mike stroked her hands and watched her closely, a look of tenderness mixed with determination on his face. He had a point. A scene with him would help her release her tension without having to admit her innermost thoughts. She could use a good beating right about now.

"Okay," she conceded. "The more intense the scene, the better."

"Good. Now I want you on your stomach on the bed. I'll be right back."

"My toys are in a black bag in the closet," she told him as she got into position.

But he didn't go into the closet. He went into the bathroom and returned with some body lotion she'd had sitting on the counter.

"What are you doing? I thought you said you'd beat me?"

"Ssshhh. No talking from now on unless I ask you a question. To clarify, I said I could help you with your tension. I didn't say I'd beat you."

"But I want a beating! That's why I said yes!"

He swatted her firmly on the ass and she raised it for more. But one was all she got. "Now, be quiet and let me do my job, which is to help you relax."

Fine! She'd allow him leeway for a few minutes to see what he'd do, but she wouldn't let it go on too long if he was just going to give her a simple massage.

He climbed onto the bed and straddled her waist. He squirted some lotion onto his hands, rubbed them together to warm it then started to massage her shoulders. These weren't tender strokes. His fingers gripped her muscles and pressed hard, causing a blessed pain that coursed through her, reaching the core of her distress. At the point at which she would feel she couldn't take it anymore he'd move to another spot, kneading the knots in her muscles until they relented and softened. By the time he made his way down to her toes, she was a pile of goo. She wasn't sure she'd even be able to get up. She thought she felt him kiss her shoulder before she wandered into a stupor.

Mike was grateful when Sam fell asleep. He could wait for the details of what had happened tonight. It was more important that she calm down and get a good rest. He'd be there when she woke, and they could talk then.

He sat in a chair by the bed. As much as he wanted to wrap her in his arms, he wouldn't presume to lie next to her without her acknowledgment. They still had a long way to go before he could take those kinds of liberties. And yet nothing would have thrilled him more than holding her tightly against him and providing the warmth and comfort that he was sure she needed.

He must have dozed off himself because the next thing he knew there was light in the room. A glance at the bedside clock showed seven o'clock. Sam was still sprawled on the bed just like he'd left her, assuring him she was in a deep sleep. *Good. She needed it.*

He got up and went into the living room to call his office and leave a message for his secretary Elaine that he'd be in late. Then he went into the kitchen to brew coffee and make breakfast. It didn't take long before he had two cups of coffee on a tray with scrambled eggs and toast. He was about to bring them into the bedroom when Sam appeared in the kitchen doorway.

Surprisingly, she was naked. Not that seeing her without clothes was unusual. She never seemed to be self-conscious walking around nude in the club. But she'd grabbed for a robe last night when she'd wanted to put distance between them, hence his surprise at her nakedness now. It was a good sign. Maybe she was ready to open up to him.

"I thought I smelled coffee and eggs. Thank you for making breakfast."

"How did you know I made eggs? I can understand smelling the coffee but eggs…?"

She smiled at him in amusement. "It's not really the eggs but the cooking butter I smelled. My extraordinary training as a chef allowed me to make the inevitable leap to eggs."

"Learn something new every day. Come, sit down and eat before everything gets cold."

She sat down at the breakfast bar and he placed her eggs and coffee in front of her.

"Thank you. I'm starving."

"You had an eventful evening. Took a lot of your energy."

She didn't answer. She waited for him to sit then began to eat.

"So? Does the chef approve of my cooking?"

She nodded as she took a bite of toast. "Mmhmm."

"I'm proud of myself if I can impress a chef. Though I have to admit scrambled eggs is one of the few dishes in my repertoire. I don't cook very much."

"I'm not surprised. Men aren't taught how to cook and that's a shame. Particularly since men are living alone till a much older age these days. It's not that hard to learn the basics so you can survive without having to eat takeout all the time."

He raised his eyebrows. "I could never cook like you. I'd never have the patience."

After a long sip of coffee, she said, "I could teach you stuff that wouldn't tax the patience of even the most impatient person. And you would like what you make."

He really wasn't that interested in learning how to cook—he wasn't that particular about what he ate. But if it meant she'd spend more time with him outside the dungeon, he was willing to give it a chance.

"Okay. When would you like the lessons to start?"

She laughed, a full joyful laugh, one that lit up her face and seemed to erase all the tension from the night before. "I didn't think you'd actually take me up on the offer."

Disappointment crashed in on him, but he schooled his expression so that she wouldn't know. "That's fine. I know you don't have a lot of free time to spend teaching me."

She reached out to brush her hand along his arm. "I didn't mean to tease you. I really was surprised by your saying yes. I think I can find the time to do it. Unless we have a huge event on the weekend we don't start most party prep before Wednesday. I'm usually off Monday and sometimes Tuesday. I think it could be fun."

He didn't realize he was holding his breath until the air started to seep into his lungs again. He wasn't sure when he'd become so invested in spending time with her, but he knew now that he wanted to whenever he could. She brought a brightness into his world he only now noticed had been lacking.

"As long as I'm not working either, those nights would be good for me."

"So what's your favorite meal?"

He hesitated. "You're going to laugh. Even though I grew up with an Irish background, my mother's best dish was meatballs and spaghetti. It's still my favorite."

"You and most of the rest of the New Jersey. That should be our first lesson."

"Deal." He reached out to shake on it before she could change her mind once she realized what kind of time commitment it would be. "Are you free tonight? I should be done at work by five."

Just as he thought, the minute it hit her that she'd committed to seeing him again so soon, she became a bit reluctant. He watched the battle play over her expressive face and knew the minute he'd won.

"Okay. I'll go shopping for the ingredients and you can meet me back here when you're done. I'm assuming your kitchen isn't that well-equipped."

"You'd be right in that assumption."

She got up and cleared the dishes. He marveled at her comfort in her nakedness and took advantage of the ability to watch her breasts jiggle as she put the dishes in the dishwasher. Then he got to ogle her ass as she stood in front of the sink and washed the frying pan. It was a beautiful display of the female form, and he had to admonish his dick at getting too excited from watching her bend over to put the frying pan back in the lower cabinet. Given the events of the previous evening, he wasn't going to try to assuage his hunger to fuck her long and hard. She wasn't ready, and he would hold back till she was.

Finished with her chores, Sam sauntered off toward the bedroom. "I'm going to get dressed so I can go shopping."

"I should be going," he called after her retreating form. She pivoted and returned, wrapping her arms around him.

"Thank you for last night. You were right. I did need someone, and I appreciate that you insisted on staying. The massage was incredible, and I know I slept better because of it."

He hugged her tightly, breathing in her glorious scent, which further challenged his self-control.

"It was my pleasure. I hope one day you'll trust someone enough to tell them why you were in such pain. It's not good to keep that bottled up inside."

To his dismay, she pulled away from him. "You're right, but it's probably not going to happen."

At least not now. But someday...

Chapter Six

Mike was finishing up his last call when his secretary informed him that his buddy Derek was waiting to see him. Mike had her send him in.

Derek looked worn and tired. The toll of having his daughter mixed up with a creep was clearly weighing on him.

"Hey, man, you look terrible," Mike told him after he settled in the chair. "I'm going to assume you haven't heard from Cassie?"

"Nah. My wife hasn't slept since she left, and I've been worried sick as well. I wanted to know if you have any news."

Mike had news, but he was reluctant to tell Derek. It wasn't good. "I've spoken to my contacts at the police precinct near where they operate and six of the Pagans were picked up after a battle with another gang they're having a turf war with. The feeling around the precinct is that the war is ramping up and the cops are preparing for a full-scale conflagration."

"Fuck! That can't be good. It means anyone associated with the Pagans becomes a target, including Cassie!"

Derek jumped up and started to pace.

"I know it looks bad, but we still have to tread cautiously," Mike warned.

"Maybe we'll get lucky and someone will take out the fucker and Cassie will be forced to come home." Derek stopped in front of Mike's desk. "You have to get her out of there before she gets killed. This is really serious now."

Mike regarded his friend with a look he hoped was sympathetic.

"I've got a number of people watching out for her in different places where the Pagans hang out. If there's a chance I can get to her without tipping off Frankie, I will. You have to go home and take care of your wife."

"I'm not sure I can sit around much longer not doing anything."

Crap! He couldn't have Derek going off half-cocked in desperation looking for Cassie. He'd only get himself killed.

"Listen, man, I promise I'll keep you informed if anything happens. I know you can take care of yourself in battle, but this is very different. Give me a few more days to make something happen."

Derek sighed long and hard then nodded. "A few more days. Then I'm going to hunt the son of a bitch down, and I won't be responsible for what happens to him."

As Mike led Derek out, he again promised to keep Derek up to date. He then made another round of calls to find out if Cassie had been spotted in any of the Pagan haunts.

* * * *

Sam arranged all the ingredients for the meatballs and spaghetti on her large kitchen counter then settled into her favorite living room chair to wait for Mike and look through her newest cookbook, *Noma*. It was out-of-this-world cooking by a world-class chef that appealed to her sense of adventure, and she was soon lost in the fabulous food shots and interesting dishes. It was only after her phone rang that she realized Mike was more than an hour late.

"I'm so sorry, Sam, but I had to check out some places for a client. I'm on my way and should be there in a half hour. I hope I didn't screw things up too much."

"No, but I think I'll take care of a few of the preliminaries so it doesn't get too late before we eat."

"Whatever you have to do is fine with me. See you soon."

She hung up and went back into the kitchen to chop the onions, garlic and herbs that she had laid out. She opened the cans of tomatoes, squeezed the tomatoes through her hands to break them down and tore up the day-old bread to be soaked in milk. By the time he rang the doorbell she had most of the prep work done, had made a salad and set out the pans she was going to use.

Mike looked frazzled when he arrived. His hair was askew, probably from his habit of running his hands anxiously through it, and frown lines creased his face. Once inside, he tried to paste on a smile, but she caught on to his distress.

"What's wrong? You look like you've been through the wringer."

"Is it that obvious? I usually have a pretty good poker face."

She sidled up to him till she was barely touching him. "If that's your poker face, I'm ready to put down at least a thousand for a game."

He laughed and pulled her into an embrace. "Be careful. It could be my way of enticing you into a game. I don't usually lose."

She kissed him softly and nibbled on his lower lip. "I don't either," she whispered in challenge.

He hugged her tighter and gave her a swift swat on her ass. "Okay, you're on. Only we're not going to be playing poker. And I think it's a game we both can win. I want you to undress and wear only your chef's jacket and apron. That way it will be safe for you to cook, but I'll get to watch your delightful ass."

"Aren't you going to help me?"

He kissed her quickly and replied, "If you don't mind, I'd rather watch. I'll see what you're doing so I can do it next time."

She extricated herself from his hold and began a slow striptease. He leaned up against the door and smiled as he watched each piece of clothing fall to the floor. When she was completely naked, she went into the kitchen, put on her chef's coat and apron and twirled for his amusement, her raised arms pulling up the jacket to completely reveal her ass.

"Very nice. Now cook for me, woman! I've had a hard day." He moved into the kitchen and sat at the counter while she prepared the meal.

"Do you want to talk about it?" she asked as she mixed the meat with the herbs, the egg, the soaked bread and the breadcrumbs.

"Unfortunately there's not a lot to tell. My buddy's daughter has run off with a motorcycle gang member and I can't seem to locate her. If anything happens to her, I'll never forgive myself."

"You can't be responsible if she does something stupid," Sam declared as she scooped and rolled the meatballs.

"She's only nineteen. Didn't you ever do anything stupid when you were that young?"

Sam stopped scooping, the vision of herself cowering under Alex's control overwhelming her. She'd been older than nineteen and had still been so, so stupid. A wave of nausea assaulted her and she moved to one of the counter stools to sit down.

"Is it what's been haunting you since that bastard showed up at the restaurant?"

She nodded and decided to come clean.

"I had a bad D/s relationship with Alex, that's the asshole's name, many years ago. He pushed me into a tiny box until I couldn't breathe and it took me way too long to wrangle myself out of it. He alienated me from my friends and family to the point I was totally dependent on him. When I got the courage to leave, he made it so unpleasant. It took me a long time to feel myself again and to have a sense of well-being. I still have a hard time believing that I let someone do that to me, that I was so naïve and weak."

With a sigh, she rested her head on her hands on the counter. Mike threaded his hand through her hair and gently forced her to turn into him. He encircled her in his arms.

"And that's why you don't want to submit, isn't it?"

She looked up at him, unexpected anger bubbling up inside her. "I will never allow someone to take away my autonomy like that again!"

He ran his hands along her arms in a soothing gesture. "I get it. But that has nothing to do with true submission. I would never ask you to give up control without the option of your taking it back at any time. That's a genuine power exchange. What you had with Alex was abuse, and I think you know it, intellectually if not emotionally."

"Maybe I do, but I'm not taking any chances of it happening again. As the expression goes, 'Fool me once, shame on you. Fool me twice, shame on me'."

He stroked her lightly as they talked, and she had the feeling he was trying to persuade her with his touch that she knew better.

"First of all, you're not young and naïve anymore. It's highly unlikely that anyone could seduce you down that road again. You're savvy enough to see the red flags before you get too far. Second, trust takes time to develop. For you I guess it will take even more. But I hope you'll at least keep an open mind. The minute something doesn't work for you, you have to tell me. It's a two-way street. I have to trust that you'll let me know when you're uncomfortable."

She didn't answer. She wasn't ready to accede to anything that resembled a relationship, even though the desire to let him into her life was stronger than anything she'd felt since Alex. He appealed to her submissive side, and she was tempted to put herself into his Dominant care. He wasn't Alex in any way, shape or form, but her heart had been sealed shut and it would take more than a promise of safety for her to completely open up to anyone again.

"I'm not asking for a commitment now," Mike asserted. "I'm not even going to offer you a play collar. I just want you to keep an open mind, to allow things to flow naturally. As I said, the minute you're not comfortable, you let me know. That's it for now, okay?"

She gave him the best smile she could, which turned out to be somewhat cockeyed, but he smiled back with enthusiasm, apparently accepting her half-assed conciliation.

"So, I think you should get back to cooking or we're not going to eat tonight, are we?"

"Crap!" Sam jumped up and rounded the counter. She poured oil into her cast iron pan then filled up her stockpot with water and set it to boil.

"Have I told you how much I love looking at your delectable ass?" Mike asked as she moved about.

"You have." She playfully shook it at him.

"I just wanted to make sure you understood how much I'm enjoying watching you cook in that outfit. I may have to interrupt the cooking before it's finished to assuage my need. I'm not sure I'll be able to last through dinner."

She turned to him before placing the meatballs in the hot oil. "Once these go into the pan, there's no stopping," she warned.

"Turn off the flame and come here for a minute. Then you can finish the job."

She obeyed his command willingly, feeling the pull of his dominance but also feeling safe within its confines. He pointed to the floor and she knelt before him and watched as he unzipped his pants. Given all the time he had spent ensuring her pleasure, she was more than happy to give him this. As he leaned against the counter and nodded, she reached in and embraced his cock. After a few strokes she pulled it free and leaned forward to give it a lick.

"Don't tease or you won't be happy with the consequences. I want you to suck me off hard and fast and make me come quickly. I'm hungry in more ways than one."

Fine. She could do that. In fact, she was really good at it.

As Sam eased her mouth over his cock, Mike settled in. He allowed her to rest her arms on his thighs instead of putting them behind her back, where he usually liked his subs to keep them. He enjoyed the challenge of making them use only their mouths to pleasure him. But if he was going to force Sam to be quick, it was only fair to allow her the ability to anchor herself against him. And if she used her hands to finish the job, that worked too.

Which was exactly what she did. She grabbed the base of his shaft and pumped it while she sucked the head, making sure to tease the underside with her tongue. It didn't take long before he was spurting down her throat, the release robbing his body of its strength and relaxing every muscle. She grinned up at him in triumph.

"Well done. I'll just stay collapsed on this stool while you finish cooking. At the moment I'm not good for anything else."

She giggled, actually giggled like a little girl, and he was floored by the genuine, unguarded moment. There were layers here, layers she kept so shielded that when she peeled them back it was delightful. It made him want it all, right down to the center of her soul.

She gave him a quick kiss on the tip of his cock and a big smile before she rose to finish cooking. He restrained himself from patting her on the head, remembering that the last time he'd done that, it hadn't worked out so well.

She was poetry in motion at the stove. The meatballs sizzled after she placed them in the hot oil. She sautéed minced onion and garlic then threw in the tomatoes to make a sauce. After she seasoned the sauce, she turned the meatballs. The smell was heavenly, so reminiscent of the smell of his mother's kitchen that it almost brought tears to his eyes. He couldn't wait to taste her creation.

She hummed while she cooked, accompanying her song with an occasional shimmy. It took him off guard to see her so relaxed and happy, a stark contrast to the carefully controlled woman he had first met. He was sorry he hadn't backed up her punch to Alex's face with one of his own. It would have made him feel better to know he had helped avenge her, but he had to admit she had done pretty well on her own. He hoped one day she would let him in enough to allow him to give her support so that she didn't feel she had to face the world alone. He had learned to allow others to help him out on the battlefield, and it made such a difference in the way he approached his life now. His buddies reached out to him and he relied on them in return. A relationship between a man and a woman could be the same way, each made stronger by the support of the other. Sam could be the perfect partner for him if he could just make her see it. *Patience, man. Give it time.*

By the time everything was done, Mike was salivating. Sam placed the platter of spaghetti and meatballs on the dining table then pulled a bottle of Chianti Classico off her wine rack and handed it to him.

"Would you do the honors?" she asked, giving him a corkscrew.

He was pleasantly surprised. Despite her efficiency, she was willing to allow him this gesture of completing the service of the meal. As he opened the wine, she pulled a salad from the fridge and dressed it, then set the table. After lighting a set of candles, she stood back while he poured. She then extended her arm.

"Please be seated, Sir."

More surprises. He was pleased by the honorific, but she was still in control, and it was time to turn the tables. He shook his head and pulled out a chair.

"After you."

She sat without argument and waited until he sat before asking, "May I serve you?"

"I'd like that very much. This dinner looks amazing."

He handed her his plate, onto which she carefully twirled a mound of spaghetti along with three absolutely round meatballs. He took an exaggerated sniff of the plate as she passed it back to him, eliciting a lilting laugh from her. She put the same amount on her plate, and as soon as she was finished, he dug in.

It was everything he'd imagined and more. The spaghetti was perfectly al dente, the sauce piquant but smooth, and the meatballs were tender but flavorful. His memory of his mother's was good, but he was sure it didn't compare to this. He was halfway through the plate when he looked up to find Sam grinning at him.

"What?"

"You haven't said a word since you dipped your fork into the food. I was wondering when you'd remember I was here."

He hadn't thought he was the kind of man who blushed, but somehow his face felt warm. "Sorry," he murmured.

She reached across the table and took his hand. "Don't be. The greatest compliment you can give a chef is to get lost in a plate of their food. I'm thrilled you're enjoying it."

"I certainly am. And I think once I'm finished, I'll give you your reward for taking such good care of me."

Now it was her turn to blush. She lowered her eyelids in a beautiful suggestion of submission and a rosy flush covered her cheeks. Mike gently pulled her toward him. Without prompting, she raised her lips for a kiss. He didn't disappoint her, gently gliding his lips across hers, brushing them back and forth against the soft satiny surface before he nipped her lower lip. As she tried to pull back, he whispered, "Stay," and she pressed her lips back against his. *Yes!*

To reward her obedience, he took the offended lip into his mouth and tongued it lightly to soothe the hurt.

"Mmmm," came her breathy response.

"Just as delicious as the meal," he responded. He drew back. "I think I'll finish the food before I feast on you."

"Sounds like a plan, Sir."

She sat back and watched with shining eyes as he plunged his fork back into his food then took a bite of meatball. "Mmmmm," he said with almost the same inflection as she'd had when uttering that sound. "Best I ever had."

"Then you haven't been to Italy," she countered.

"No, I haven't. But I'm sure this is as good as any I could find there."

"Well, I will admit I learned how to make meatballs from an Italian grandma who used to live near me when I was younger. So there is an authenticity to them."

"I like them. And I'm going to eat every bit on my plate." He popped another bite into his mouth and groaned. "So good!"

She was excited he was enjoying her food. Not that she didn't have confidence in her ability to make meatballs and spaghetti. But this was so much more personal than feeding customers or even bringing food to a party. As she ate, she surreptitiously watched him devour his food with relish. The ability to give him pleasure with her cooking brought her an unexpected joy. She had never pictured herself as a service submissive, but obviously there was an element of it lurking in the deep recesses of her psyche, and it was happy at the moment, particularly when he asked for seconds. Maybe that was why she'd become a chef in the first place.

Once they'd finished, Mike helped her clear the dishes and load the dishwasher. After packing up the leftovers, she decided to leave the pots in the sink for a soak.

"I forgot to make something for dessert. I can't believe I did that."

"I already decided I was having you for dessert, so don't worry. I want you to remove the chef coat and apron and follow me to the living room."

He walked into the living room without waiting to see if she obeyed him. But she allowed him that confidence because she wanted to follow his lead — at least for now.

He was sitting on the sofa when she walked in.

"Come sit next to me so we can talk."

He patted the sofa and she plopped down next to him. He reached over and pulled her legs over his lap and she settled comfortably against the sofa arm.

"I'd like to try a true power exchange for a while, where I don't have to wrestle you for control. It won't be a very active play scene. I'd like to work on building trust. As always, you'll have your safeword, and any time you feel like you want to opt out I'll respect your wishes. Do you think you can do that? Be truly submissive and not merely a bottom for me?"

She closed her eyes and leaned her head back. *Ugh! Can't we just play and build trust that way?* He was really pushing her past her comfort zone. Did she want to go there? *Can I?*

Mike remained silent, his only movement gently smoothing his hand up and down her calves. He didn't make any attempt to pressure her into it. He'd made his case and he was giving her all the time she needed to make a decision. If she said no, she suspected they would proceed with their evening play. He didn't threaten to leave or withhold himself from her.

Without warning, Sam's emotions overwhelmed her. She was near tears, and it annoyed the hell out of her. She realized this *was* what she wanted, had wanted since before she'd met Alex. He'd ruined it for her, but now she was with a man who wanted to make it right. She wanted to let go so much she could taste it. But every time she tried to say yes, the word wouldn't come out of her mouth.

"Hey, it's okay. We don't have to do it now. Or ever, for that matter. I was hoping for it, but it won't keep me from seeing you, Sam."

"I think I want it too." Sam sat up and met his gaze. "I don't know why I'm having such a hard time saying yes."

"You're still frightened. And I get it. But I need 'yes' to proceed. I can only promise that the minute it doesn't work for you anymore, or that you're too anxious about what's happening, we'll stop immediately."

Without further rumination, she uttered "Yes". His answering smile lit up his whole face. He continued to stroke her legs. Now that she'd said yes, she became somewhat fidgety in anticipation of his next move.

"Sit still and relax," he instructed.

"Not easy," she murmured. "I'm a bit wound up."

"Okay. Let's try this. I want you to take a pillow from the sofa and kneel on it right here in front of me. Thighs open wide, hands resting on your thighs, eyes down."

He pointed to a spot between his legs. She looked at the spot, frozen for a moment. It wasn't as though she hadn't knelt before while a Dom was preparing a station for play. However, this was different. This was presenting herself to him as a submissive. But there was no time like the present to give it a go. She got up, grabbed a pillow and settled on it just as he asked. He didn't say a word while she positioned herself properly. Once she was ready, he began to stroke her head, then moved his hands down the sides of her face and rested them lightly around her neck.

"You have no idea how beautiful you look, my lovely girl."

At his words, Sam's anxiety diminished and she settled farther back onto her heels.

"That's it. Relax. Feel my admiration, my respect. Let me care for you, which is different from taking care of you. I know you can do that for yourself."

His voice was low but firm, his direction forceful. Sam's emotions continued to churn the more she gave herself up to him. He pulled her forward, directing her with his hands to rest her head on his thigh and sit. He moved his other leg so that it pressed against her, cocooning her between his legs. He never stopped stroking her, and eventually she felt her heartbeat slow to a normal pace.

It felt better than she had anticipated. Once she settled, she allowed herself to experience the full force of his attention. He was focused solely on her, her needs, her comfort. She couldn't remember the last time she'd felt so safe, so nurtured. Not since her childhood.

"Would you like to watch a movie?"

"What?"

"A movie. You know, moving pictures. They were started in the 1920s."

She looked up at him, incredulous. "That's what you want to do now? I thought we were in a scene."

"We are, my lovely girl. You're going to sit here at my feet and we're going to enjoy a movie together."

"If that's what you want..."

She didn't understand, but she was letting him take control and if that's what he wanted... He reached over to the end table, picked up the remote and turned on the TV, scrolling through the Netflix offerings.

"Holy cow. *Into the Night*. Funny, funny movie. Have you ever seen it?"

"No."

"Then we'll watch this. I think you'll enjoy it."

He started the movie and sat back, gently directing her to turn to face the screen with her back against the sofa. He closed his legs so she was once again enclosed in his body heat. He gathered her long hair and splayed it out so that he could run his fingers through it, laughing when she let out a long sigh.

"Good?"

"Yes, Sir. Very good."

Am I ever. Who would have thought sitting quietly at his feet as he played with her hair and stroked her while they watched Jeff Goldblum and Michelle Pfeiffer race frantically through the night fleeing four mad criminals would make her feel so peaceful. She had never spent time with a man that felt like this. Ever.

Mike couldn't believe she hadn't moved or protested since he'd placed her on the floor at his feet. He had expected at least a little blowback, but she seemed to have acclimated herself to her situation after only a little bit of fidgeting. He had suspected her submissive side was deeply ingrained, but he hadn't expected her to give over to him so completely.

Maybe it was the camaraderie of the laughter at the movie that distracted her from the elemental nature of her position. The telling moment would happen now that it was over. Would she wait for his direction or get up on her own accord?

Incredibly, she waited. He clicked off the television and bent down to kiss her on the top of her head.

"It looked like you enjoyed the movie, yes?"

She nodded. He pulled her hair firmly and she gave him the proper response. "Yes, Sir, I did."

"The next question is a bit more probing. Did you enjoy watching the movie sitting at my feet?"

He didn't make her turn and face him to answer. He hoped that if she didn't have to look him in the eyes, to reveal herself so intimately, that she might be truthful with him.

She didn't respond immediately, and he waited her out. He wanted her to think about it, to realize that she was comfortable at his feet. He'd felt her relax fairly quickly after the movie started. She leaned forward, away from his touch.

"I don't like to admit it, but it was nice. I was calm in a way I hadn't anticipated. Yeah...it was nice."

"Can I ask why you moved away from me to say that?"

She didn't move back into position, but she turned to look at him, a pained expression on her face.

"You don't let up, do you? You want to make me bare my soul. I don't like it."

She turned back away from him, leaning her head against her own knees. He considered letting it all go for now, allowing her to retreat and trying another time. But he decided against it. If they were going to work, they had to figure out the parameters of their relationship.

"Why don't you like it? We didn't do anything that significant. We basically sat and enjoyed each other's company. We just did it with me in charge. I didn't push you into anything you didn't want to do, did I?"

A very soft, "No."

Not acceptable. Their power exchange wouldn't work if she didn't face her fears.

"Sam, I want you to get up and sit on the couch with me for a few moments. We have to talk and I need you to be comfortable but to face me when we do this."

She slowly rose then plopped herself down next to him like a petulant child. He raised an eyebrow at her. She had the good grace to blush.

"Honesty, Sam. You've been in the lifestyle long enough to know it's the only way this works. Now, I need you to tell me, clearly and without evasion, how this experience made you feel."

She leaned back against the arm of the sofa and crossed her arms in a gesture that seemed designed to create a barrier between them. He believed it was an attempt to get a rise out of him and divert attention from the question. He wasn't buying into it.

"I'm waiting, Sam. And I can wait for a very long time. I've had stakeouts that have lasted days."

"Look, you talk about not pushing me past my comfort zone. Well, talking about feelings is way out of my comfort zone. I can take all kinds of pain and be fine. Just don't ask me what I'm feeling."

He shook his head, working hard to contain a wry smile. "Sorry, my lovely girl, but this is where it all gets real. If you don't tell me how you feel, then we have nothing. I don't think that's what you want, is it?"

She uncrossed her arms, raised her knees and wrapped her arms around them, creating a bigger barrier, but she rested her chin on her knees and looked him straight in the eyes.

"I don't think so either... I liked it very much... You make me feel...cherished. I don't think I've ever felt cherished by a man."

"I do cherish you and your submission to me. I will never take it for granted because I know it takes such a leap of faith for you to give it to me."

"God, does it ever!"

He laughed at her spontaneous remark while she looked at him in distress. "Did I say that out loud?"

"Yup. And it's okay because it's your real feelings."

She rolled her eyes at him.

"I mean it. Now I would like to take you to bed and make love to you."

"I'm not a big fan of vanilla sex. Kink is what gets me off."

"I didn't say anything about vanilla sex. I was talking about a connection between the two of us. If you don't want it, say no. But I will not have sex with you right now without that connection."

He stood up and held out his hand. She didn't wait long before she put her hand in his and let him help her up. He pulled her up against him, hugging her. Her whimper of acquiescence stirred up his protective instincts. He was ready to take her on, to possess her, to let her know that he was there for her in any way she could need him.

He pressed his lips against her neck and she offered her throat. His body hummed in tune with hers, his heartbeat following the rhythm of the artery pulsing in her neck. He kissed her, then skimmed his teeth back and forth over her skin before taking a quick nip of her flesh. Her breath hitched in response as she sank farther into his arms.

"Come with me." He took her hand and led her down the hall. When they reached her bedroom, he turned to her. "Do you have any rope?"

"In the bottom drawer of the dresser."

"Pull down the covers and get into bed spread-eagled."

As she did as he directed, he opened the dresser drawer. To his delight, in addition to rope, there was a treasure trove of toys. He selected a pair of nipple clamps and a few hanks of deep red rope. The color would look enticing against her olive skin.

He smiled as he approached the bed. "Where's the Hitachi?"

She pointed to the bedside table. He removed it then asked playfully, "Were you a Girl Scout? You're awfully prepared."

"If you don't provide what you want, you won't get what you want," she retorted with a smirk.

"When was the last time someone used these things on you?"

That wonderful blush he was growing fond of seeing appeared on her cheeks. She didn't answer.

"Sam, I need you to tell me the truth. Answer me."

"I've never had a man in this bedroom before."

Holy fuck! "Really?"

"Really. I play in the club."

"So what are these for?" He glanced down at the toys. Her blush intensified.

"Self-pleasure. I've never used the rope."

"Well, it's time to remedy that. I'll be in charge of your pleasure this evening. Let me have your hands."

She offered them up and he bound them together in a rope cuff, brought her hands over her head and secured the rope to the headboard. He then tied a cuff around one ankle, pulled her leg wide and brought the rope under the mattress around to the opposite side, securing her other leg open. Without his prompting, she settled into position.

Sitting down on the bed, he began to caress her, starting with her face. He smoothed his hands down the sides of her cheeks, pausing to graze his fingers over her lips. She tried to suck his fingers into her mouth, but he shook his head.

"Uh-uh," he admonished. "You follow my lead. Relax and feel. I will tell you if I want you to move. Am I clear?"

She nodded. He pinched her nipple hard and she gave him the "Yes, Sir!" he required. He went back to caressing her, his hands roaming over her collarbone, down her breasts, teasing her with his palms, fondling her nipples. She tried to press her nipples more firmly against him but he pulled his hands away. Her complaint was vocal.

"Aaaaahhhh. We already went through this, only last time you made *me* stroke my nipples. You're torturing me! Please, I need more."

"You'll get it when *I'm* ready, and not before."

He resumed trailing his fingers over her body, circling her belly then moving over her mound. Her butt muscles contracted, but she didn't complain further. A brief pass over her labia assured him she was wet. His own excitement revved up in response, his dick pressing against the zipper of his pants. *Down, boy! We're going to concentrate on her first.*

He bent forward and sucked a nipple into his mouth, eliciting a full gasp from her. He swirled his tongue over the tip in a rhythmic motion and she began to purr. He moved to the other nipple, laving it in the same manner while he applied gradual pressure to the first one. Her answering growl made him smile against her breast.

He sat back up and grabbed the Hitachi, turning it on low and pressing it against her already abraded nipple. Her head lolled back in pleasure. Alternating sides, he placed the machine against her over and over until she cried out, "Please, Sir, may I come?"

"Yes, lovely girl, you may."

Her body immediately began to undulate, her head rocking back and forth, a guttural moan emitting from her throat. He continued contact with her nipples until she sank back into the bed and stopped moving except for the rapid rise and fall of her chest. He planted gentle kisses over her closed eyes and her cheeks.

"Thank you, Sir," she told him as she began to catch her breath.

"It is definitely my pleasure. Let's try for another one." Her eyes opened wide, but she didn't protest. "That's my lovely girl."

He smiled wickedly at her as he picked up the nipple clamps. Her pussy clenched in anticipation. Her nipples were overly sensitized now — those clamps were going to hurt.

She steeled herself against the assault, but it only made it worse when he attached the first clamp. The agony seared her chest and she couldn't help crying out.

"Fuck, that hurts!"

"Is that a bad hurt or a good one?" Mike sat and watched her. She catalogued her feelings. Her nipple throbbed, but so did her clit, and not in a bad way. Then the pain in her nipple slowly dissipated to numbness. She knew when he took the clamps off the suffering would return a hundredfold, but for now all she felt were the pulsations of pleasure in her clit.

"Good until you put the other one on."

"And it will get good as well, won't it?"

"Yes, Sir...eventually."

"Enduring pain to reach pleasure is part of what this is about, isn't it?" He smoothed his hand over her breast, securing her nipple between his fingers, but he didn't put on the clamp until she responded.

"Yes, Sir, it is."

He nodded and secured the clamp. She cried out once more and continued to whimper until the numbness took hold. By then she felt her clit would explode. The juxtaposition of the grips of the clamps against her nipples and the lack of attention to her clit was a bit crazy-making. She looked to Mike in desperation.

"Please, Sir..."

He didn't force her to elucidate. He picked up the Hitachi and put it right where she felt desperate for touch. *So good. So, so good.* He didn't move it around, just continued to push the fat head of the machine up against her. She raised her hips to increase the pressure.

"You may come whenever it hits you," he told her as he adjusted the button to high. She went over like a firecracker, shattering into an intense orgasm. The shots of pain caused by the clamps attached to her quivering breasts only intensified the feeling. She was wrung out when she came down.

"You have no idea how much pleasure you give me when I watch you come apart from my efforts."

He pushed her hair back from her face and once again caressed her cheeks. As her breathing came back to normal, she realized she was parched.

"May I have some water, Sir? There are bottles in the fridge."

"Of course. I'll be right back."

He got up quickly and almost ran down the hall. She was grateful to have a moment to compose herself without being under his watchful eye. He had read her every movement, every expression on her face. Nothing got past him because he paid such close attention. He was so intense, yet it didn't frighten her like it usually did. She still felt safe with him, and it was kind of miraculous.

When he returned, he put his hand under her head and supported her while he lifted the water to her lips. She drank in huge gulps, not caring that some of it spilled on her breasts. When she nodded, he put the bottle down and went into the bathroom to get a towel. He gently wiped the water away, being careful not to pull on the clamps.

"I think it's time they came off. Are you ready?"

"Yes, Sir," she told him as she tensed against what she knew was going to be searing pain.

He leaned over her, and as soon as he removed a clamp he sucked on her nipple, laving it firmly with his tongue, massaging away the torment. He did the same with the other one. By the time he was done she was back on the edge of overstimulation.

He placed the clamps next to the Hitachi on the night table. Removing his clothes revealed his own excitement. She drank in his beautiful body, which was not diminished at all by the scar that continued down to the middle of his chest. She wanted to know how he got it, but now was not the time. She wanted to revel in the beauty of his muscular body and the sight of his thick long cock pointing proudly upward. She salivated a bit as she watched him slide a condom over his length. She needed that cock inside her as soon as possible.

"Fuck me, please, Sir."

"No, but I will make love to your beautiful body and the soul that lives inside it."

"How did you become such a romantic?"

"I'm inspired by you, my lovely girl. Now *ssshhh*. The only sounds I want to hear from you are sounds of ecstasy."

He crawled up between her legs, settling his full weight over her as he held her in his embrace. He pressed his cock against her entrance and slowly entered, rocking in and out until he was fully seated.

"Look at me, Sam. Don't close your eyes."

She was enveloped by him, inside and out, almost to the point of suffocation. Almost. He was taking her, fully and completely, and he was looking into the core of her being while he gave her the greatest pleasure she had ever known. And for the first time since Alex, she wasn't panicked. She felt protected, his strength comforting, his power soothing. She let go and gave him her all.

He stroked her slowly but firmly, moving till he found that spot that intensified her pleasure, continuing till the sensation overwhelmed her and she went over, awash in ecstasy, her keening cry proclaiming her rapture.

Her next awareness was of Mike smiling down at her.

"Are you okay? I think I lost you there for a moment."

He was still pressed against her from head to toe, still inside her.

"Sorry."

"I'm fine, Sam. I came when you did, but I don't think you were aware of anything during that intense orgasm, which milked me dry with its force. I'm just not ready to leave the comfort of your body yet. Is that all right?"

"You feel really good inside me. I'm not sure I'll ever want you to leave."

He pressed a gentle kiss. on her forehead. "You have no idea how happy that makes me, my lovely girl. But it's time to get you untied."

With that, he rose, and she felt the loss acutely. He untied her with dispatch, and before she could really get cold he was back beside her, turning them so she was cocooned in his embrace.

It was a comforting feeling, having him pressed against her. She burrowed against his chest, trying to get even closer. Squeezing her he kissed her on top of her head. As her heartbeat slowed, she realized a sense of calm had descended on her, wrapping her in a cloak of peacefulness. Another new experience.

The silence between them lengthened, but it wasn't awkward. His arms, his body provided a feeling of serenity she reveled in. It could go on forever and she wouldn't mind. The aftermath was what worried her. Would he try to control her more now that they had brought their relationship to a new level? Would he feel proprietary over her?

"Hey, what's wrong? You've become restless all of a sudden."

He was incredibly in tune with her, she'd give him that.

"I'm fine. I don't do warm and fuzzy very well."

"That's a shame. Enjoying the afterglow is almost as good as the act itself."

"I guess it depends on who you're with. It's never been my favorite part."

Mike pulled back a bit, compelling her to look up at him.

"I guess I'm disappointed. I had hoped ours was a bond you felt good about."

The discouragement reflected in his eyes made her feel enormously guilty. He had been nothing but careful and caring and she wasn't returning his consideration of her. She pressed against his chest before she spoke.

"It was good, Mike. It really was. And I do feel very close to you. But I'm not sure I'm cut out for long-term."

She could feel the rise and fall of his chest as he sighed deeply.

"I promise, Sam, I'm not asking for a long-term commitment, and I'm certainly not looking for a twenty-four-seven relationship, which I know scares the hell out of you. I'm just hoping for honesty between us when we're together. Is that too hard for you?"

"I guess not. I promise to try not to let my insecurities overwhelm me when we're together. You haven't done anything so far that should make me uncomfortable. It'll just take a while for me to trust fully. I'm working on it."

He hugged and kissed her again.

"I'm patient. I'd like to stay the night and sleep wrapped around you. Would that be all right with you or would you prefer I leave? I'm going to get rid of this condom and be right back. Think about what you want."

As soon as he left her bed, she knew the answer. She didn't like the emptiness she felt without him beside her. When he came back, she reached out to him.

"Please, stay."

He took her hand, kissed her palm then crawled in beside her and enveloped her once more.

"Good night, my lovely girl."

"Good night, Sir."

She snuggled up against him, soaking up the warmth of his skin, and marveled at her own response. Being up against him was better than she'd imagined. She decided she wouldn't worry about tomorrow and just enjoy today.

Chapter Seven

Sam awoke to an unaccustomed heat surrounding her. As she tried to rise, she was held back by unyielding arms.

"Don't go yet," Mike implored. "I'm not ready to get up."

He pulled her tighter, his morning wood up against her ass. It was tempting, but she had to pee and she had to get to work. She attempted to push him away with no luck.

"I have to get up now!" she insisted.

He released her immediately and she sprang up and ran to the bathroom. She peed, brushed her teeth then turned on the shower and stuck her hand in to gauge the temperature.

"Can I at least join you in the shower?"

Sam turned to find Mike leaning up against the door to the bathroom, seemingly unabashed about his cock bobbing upward, covered in a condom. He wiggled his eyebrows and smiled.

"I'll make it worth your while," he promised.

His infectious spirit — and his demanding cock — were not to be denied. And why not? He always did make it worth her while.

"Sure. But I only have girly smelling bath products."

His grin widened. "That means I'll have your smell with me all day. Suits me."

She laughed as she pushed the door of the shower open. He followed her in, closing the door behind him. In an instant she was up against the tile wall, her hands held above her, the water streaming down her hair.

"Keep your hands where I place them and don't move," he instructed.

"Yes, Sir," she replied, ceding control to him without hesitation.

He stepped back and, after soaping up his hands, began washing her, starting with her raised arms. As he rounded her body and massaged her breasts she revved up, pushing her ass out toward him, hoping to make contact with his cock. He smacked her, the sting from the wetness jointly chastising and accelerating her desire.

"Didn't I tell you not to move?"

"Yes, Sir. But — "

"No buts. You listen or you lose. Am I clear? I can stop now."

"No, please, Sir. I'm sorry."

He gave her another swat, and it took all her self-control to keep herself from rising up on her toes in response. The pain radiated out from her backside, and all she wanted was his cock to assuage the emptiness she felt inside.

He went back to washing her, pinching her nipples before moving down, slowly massaging her clit with his soapy hands. Just as she was going to beg him once more, he plunged inside her, her now wet passage ready for him. He braced himself beside her raised arms and pounded into her. Without asking permission, she went over before he did, screaming her release, and he bit into her neck as she felt him release inside her. When her knees threatened to buckle underneath her, he hugged her around her waist and held her till she recovered.

After she had caught her breath, Mike released her, peeled off the condom, threw it in the garbage, then went back to washing her. When he was done she left the shower, almost guilty that she hadn't washed him in return, but she was now running a little late, which was his fault, wasn't it?

Once dressed, she went into the kitchen and made coffee. She grabbed butter, jam and cheese from the fridge and set out some bread. She hoped he'd be okay with a quick breakfast—her usual on a work morning. She was pouring out the coffee when he came into the kitchen looking yummy, clean-shaven with his hair slicked back.

"I hope you don't mind, I opened a new razor package."

"No, of course not. Come sit and eat. I need to get going soon."

He came over to take the cup of coffee she offered, but put it back down on the counter, invading her personal space.

"Hey, stop just a moment. Let me thank you for a terrific shower and even more so, for a wonderful evening." He lifted her chin to force her to look at him. "You are an incredible woman, Sam, and I appreciate the effort you made last night to let go and give me control. It meant a lot to me."

Sam met his gaze, absorbing his praise and approval and realizing that it was important to her.

"It was an incredible night for me too. I'm not sure why you make me want to submit to you, but I do, even against my own instincts." A momentary feeling of panic sliced through her as she said it. "But as I told you, I'm not ready for any kind of long-term commitment."

"I promised not to push you beyond what you're willing to do. We'll take it slowly. But I do want to continue seeing you. Is that all right?"

"Yes. Now sit and eat or we'll have to leave hungry."

"Yes, ma'am!" He saluted and sat, grinning broadly.

She couldn't help returning his grin. She enjoyed his company, and as they ate, that feeling of peacefulness settled over her once again. Whether or not it was because she trusted him, she wasn't sure, but it was seeming more and more like she did. By the time they were done and she'd put the dishes in the dishwasher, she was sorry they had to part.

"I'll call you later," he promised. Encircling her in his arms, he kissed her breathless. "Have a good day, my lovely girl."

As she watched him go, she was already anticipating his call and the chance to be with him again.

* * * *

It took Mike a while to refocus on his job during his ride home to change. The vision of Sam on her knees, her beauty in her submission overwhelming him, was hard to erase from his mind. They had made progress.

She was opening up to him despite her reservations and tapping into her submissive nature. It had been worth his persistence, and he wasn't going to let her pull back from him again. He just had to make sure that each time he was with her, he took her only a bit further, leading her into a commitment slowly enough that she didn't panic.

Sam was the one for him. He'd known it the moment he set eyes on her. But she was skittish, so he had given her a wide berth and waited for his opportunity. Now he hoped she would continue to let him lead her where he wanted her to go and—he was now sure—she wanted to follow.

By the time he'd changed and gone to the office, he was able to turn his attention to other matters. He wrapped up two reports on cases he'd worked on and decided to get in his car and drive around the territory where the Pagans were known to hang out.

Two hours later he got the lead he was looking for. Cassie and her boyfriend Frankie had shown up at a bar he knew was a Pagan hangout. The bartender told Mike's informant that they had been on a trip to Maryland to get help from fellow Pagan members in their drug war. Frankie was pissed that no one had decided to come back to Jersey with them.

It was a great tip. Even better was the fact that the bar needed a part-time bartender. He was grateful he had gotten his bartender's certificate when he left the service. He headed over to the Towne Tavern to apply for the job.

All eyes turned to watch Mike as he entered, and they didn't stop watching till he asked for the person hiring. Then the din recommenced. The owner, Gabe Howard, greeted him warmly and had him follow him back to his office.

Mike liked Gabe immediately. He was a man comfortable in his own skin and not at all intimidated by his clientele.

"So, Mike, why do you want to be a bartender here? I'm sure you figured out that this is a bar filled with very demanding people. You're going to have to walk on eggshells with them in order not to piss them off. And it's very important to me that you don't piss them off because then they do damage to my place."

"If you don't mind me asking, Sir, why do you allow them in?"

Gabe sat back in his chair, a frown crossing his face. "I'm not sure you're the right person for the job if you're asking that question. You don't *allow* these people to do anything. They do what they want. Fortunately for me, they pay for whatever they damage and they pay their bills. I have a full bar every night, and despite their reputation, they haven't caused me much trouble. That's mostly what I'm concerned about."

"Of course," Mike responded.

"If you don't mind *me* asking, where did you get that scar?"

"Afghanistan. I'm former Special Forces."

"Impressive. I guess that means you'll probably be able to handle yourself. Why do you want the job? I'm sure there are a lot of other, more glamorous jobs you can get."

Deciding it would be better to put his cards on the table, Mike leaned forward and looked Gabe straight in the eye. "I'm going to be upfront with you, sir. I'm a private detective and I'm trying to extricate the daughter of the man who saved my life in Afghanistan. She and her boyfriend frequent the bar. I need a way to talk to her without arousing suspicion. This job will do it."

Gabe sat for a minute before answering. "I'm sure I'm going to regret this, but I'll hire you. You and your friend deserve to be rewarded for your service to this country, and if letting you be a bartender here will help do that, I'll agree. My one request is that you keep any fights out of the bar."

"You have my word. I'll keep peace as much as I can, even the arguments that have nothing to do with me."

Gabe stood up and extended his hand. "Then the job's yours. You can start tomorrow evening. Be here by six."

Mike shook Gabe's hand. "Thank you, sir. I appreciate it."

* * * *

Sam's day kept its usual hectic pace. She and Rebecca planned the week's agenda while Allegra and Mya gave the kitchen a thorough antiseptic cleaning. After they placed their vegetable and fruit orders for the next day, they all went to Restaurant Depot to pick up supplies. They needed two vans for all they bought, and it was nearly six before they were finished unpacking everything and putting it away.

Rebecca had patiently waited till they were unpacking the vans before she asked about Mike and, contrary to her usual demand for details, had settled for a brief outline of the evening and an assurance that Sam would see him again. They had already had a phone recap of her previous date, although Sam had judiciously left out the part about decking Alex at the restaurant. She wasn't ready to rehash the details of that relationship with Rebecca or anyone else.

By the time she got home, she was ready for an easy dinner, a bath, a book and bed. She was grateful she had leftovers from the previous night. All she had to do was heat them up. She pulled out a pan to heat the meatballs in the sauce and a pot to cook pasta. Everything was beginning to simmer when Mike called. Her pulse quickened as she answered the phone.

"Hi, how was your day?" she asked.

"Quite productive. I got a lot done. How about you?"

"Pretty much the same. I'm about to have leftovers from last night."

"Mmmm. Lucky you. I wish I had taken some home with me. I could use some comfort food about now."

She made the offer without even thinking. "I certainly have enough for the two of us. Would you like to come over?"

His answer was just as quick. "I'll be there in about twenty minutes."

She hung up. Book was not going to happen and bath would become a quick shower before Mike got there. But actual hot sex was far better than just reading about it, and baths were overrated. As she rushed to her bathroom, she realized she was more excited about this evening than she had been for a long time.

By the time he arrived, Sam had everything — including herself — ready. She greeted him at the door, barefoot in a short, figure-hugging dress with nothing underneath. She shimmied up against him and when he cupped her ass, his surprised but delighted expression told her she had done the right thing. Once inside, he closed the door quickly and grabbed her, kissing her with a startling passion.

"Are you hungry?" she asked after she caught her breath.

"Absolutely!" He playfully bit her neck.

"I'm talking about dinner."

"I'm not," he replied as he kissed her again. In reply she wrapped her legs around him and, without further ado, he set off for her bedroom.

"Wait! I have to turn off the flame under the pasta water."

He carried her to the kitchen, turned off the burner and set off once again for her bedroom. After laying her gently on her back on the bed, he hurriedly shed his clothes, fishing a condom out of his pocket and putting it on the end table before he helped her pull her dress over her head.

"That didn't last long. It took me more time to decide what to wear than it stayed on." She shot him a rueful grin.

"It did its job, my lovely girl, so it was time well spent."

He waggled his eyebrows as he pushed her back down and pressed himself along her body, enveloping her in his warmth. His ardor was controlled as he gently kissed around her neck and moved down to nibble on her breasts. She welcomed his touch, his affection, his passion. He was treating her as someone precious, someone special to him, and she couldn't help but return his tenderness. She hugged him then kissed the top of his head, unable to distract him from his concentration on her now-sensitive nipples.

When it seemed as though he would never move away from the object of his desire, and she felt herself on the edge, she cried out, "Please, I'm going to come if you don't stop!"

He paused long enough to tell her to come whenever she wanted and returned to his task, sending her over. She shattered and continued to tremble as he lavished more attention on her nipples.

"Okay...okay...you're relentless!" she exclaimed, laughing at his tenacity.

"'Okay' is not a safeword," he informed her. He sucked a nipple into his mouth and laved it with his tongue. The weight of his body prevented her from rising up in response.

"You're driving me crazy!" She felt like she was going to explode out of her skin as another orgasm rippled through her. "Please!" she gasped.

"Still not a safeword," he taunted. He did, however, begin to move south on her body, softly kissing his way down to her mound, parting her labia and closing his lips around her clit. His tongue stroked her over and over until she was a quivering mess.

"Come for me again!" Mike demanded, and she spasmed uncontrollably while he continued licking her.

Collapsing on the bed, she complained, "I'm not going to have enough energy to give you a turn."

"I'm not worried," he answered. He wended his way back up until he covered her whole body again and leaned over to grab the condom. He handed it to her.

"Think you could manage this?"

She rolled her eyes at him but took the condom and unwrapped it while he lay back on the bed. She placed it between her lips and rolled it on, sucking him firmly after she had it in place. He pulled her back up to his chest.

"See? You have more energy than you thought. If you'd like, you can just lie back and I'll do all the work—but I *will* make you come again."

She took him up on the deal. Flipping them over, he positioned himself at her entrance, pushed through her wetness and slammed into her, causing her to cry out. Only this time the word was "Yes!"

"I thought so." He smiled down at her as he slowly drew his cock out and pushed back in. Divine tremors rippled inside her until she felt another climax reaching for completion. He sped up only slightly, his pace keeping her on the edge but not enough to send her over.

"I want you to come with me this time," he told her. "Do you think you can do it?"

"Yes, but you have to go faster, please...Sir."

"Anything for you, lovely girl."

He sped up to a furious pace, pounding her till she couldn't hold on any longer. She clutched him tightly, her whole body reverberating with pleasure.

The next thing she knew he was kissing her gently on her eyes, her forehead, her lips. "You with me?" he asked, concern written all over his face.

"I think so. You fucked me into oblivion."

"Really? You've taken so much more from me."

She hesitated, not sure she wanted to reveal why she suspected she felt so depleted. His eyes never left hers, as though he was silently pleading with her to open up to him. Finally, she capitulated.

"My connection to you was much stronger this time. You wrung out as much intense emotion from me as you did orgasms."

He slowly brushed her lips with his then planted a soft kiss before he answered. "I'm not sorry. I care for you more than I'm sure you want to know. You've seduced me with your strength, your passion and your beauty. Now I'm hooked, and I hope to show you that you are too. We suit each other too well to turn our backs on what we have. Whether we engage in dark and intense or sweet and soft, we're a good fit."

She didn't respond. He was right, but she wasn't ready to admit it out loud even to herself.

Mike rose and went into the bathroom. After he washed up and brought out a warm cloth to wash her as well, he told her, "I want you to relax for a while. I'm going to warm the meatballs and make the pasta. You've done all the hard work already so you get to rest. I'll let you know when it's done."

She rolled over onto her side and closed her eyes. She was probably asleep before Mike hit the kitchen.

* * * *

Mike found himself dancing and singing around the kitchen as he prepared dinner, the lyrics of *I Want to Know What Love Is* reverberating in his head. When he'd become such a sap he wasn't sure, but being around Sam had certainly made him more than a little sentimental. It wasn't a feeling he was used to, but he was enjoying the hell out of it. Years of not knowing if he was going to make it out alive had taken its toll, culminating in his terrible encounter with a Taliban bayonet. Being in Sam's home, warming up a dinner she'd made for him the night before, with her resting in the bedroom after a fantastic fuck, made him feel warm and fuzzy, and he damn well wasn't going to feel ashamed about it.

He rummaged through her cabinets and found what he needed to set the table, and was about to go wake Sam when he heard her come down the hallway. She appeared in all her naked glory, a shy smile on her lips.

"Sorry I conked out on you."

"No need to apologize. I feel I've done my Dominant duty if I render you senseless." He winked at her and she laughed in return. He was smitten by the way she looked when she was happy. It was a look he wanted to be sure to keep on her face whenever he could.

"Come sit down and I'll serve you dinner." He pulled a chair out from the table.

"Oh no. You heated it up, I should serve you."

Mike walked over and planted himself in front of her. In a quiet but firm voice he said, "You will sit, and you will be gracious about it. Am I clear?" He stared her down until she lowered her eyes.

"Yes, Sir," she responded.

He stepped aside and allowed her to sit, helping to push her chair in toward the table. He stalked to the stove and brought the pasta pot to the sink, drained the noodles, put them on a platter and poured the sauce and meatballs over them. Sauce splattered all over. When he went to grab a paper towel, he looked up to find Sam doing all she could to keep from laughing.

"Not the way you'd do it, huh?" Mike asked, adding an apologetic shrug.

"No...I would have added the pasta to the pan with the sauce and the meatballs and then put it on the plate with tongs. There's serving tongs in the drawer," she instructed, clearly an attempt to keep the damage to a minimum.

He laughed. "Of course. Though in my defense, I'm a little distracted by the beautiful display of feminine pulchritude before me."

There was that blush again, the look that momentarily made her seem so innocent and girlish. He wiped the platter and brought it to the table with the tongs, kissing her when he sat down.

"I'll let you put the food on the plates to avoid another disaster."

She chuckled as she twirled the spaghetti into a mound on each plate and strategically placed the meatballs into crevices in the pasta so they wouldn't roll off when she passed the plates. He watched her perfect technique and vowed that next time he'd impress her with his prowess in the kitchen. He hoped he'd already wowed her with his prowess in the bedroom.

The food was even better the second day. It was the perfect evening—sitting with her naked at the table, eating her delicious food, having already had even more delicious sex and looking forward to some playtime before sleep. He hoped the meal would give her the energy she needed.

The conversation was casual. He loved hearing about her kitchen activities, particularly the banter among her fellow chefs. The women pushed one another to divulge their deepest secrets, and he wished he could be a fly on the wall to hear their conversations, especially the ones about him. He knew Rebecca was on his side, and he was curious as to how much Sam had revealed about their relationship. He figured the more she was willing to tell her friends about them, the more she'd accepted they were a couple. Maybe it was time to have lunch with Rebecca. He was sure she could advise him on how to permanently conquer his reluctant sub.

"So how was your day?" Sam asked, pulling him out of his ruminations.

"Pretty good, I think. I've got a nighttime job at the bar where the Pagans hang out. My friend's daughter and her boyfriend have been spotted there recently. I hope it will give me an opportunity to talk with her."

"Those guys don't seem the type to let anyone talk to their women. Sounds dangerous to me." She reached out and placed a hand on his arm in a gesture of concern.

He shrugged. "Usually bartenders get a pass. Unless I'm really persistent, I don't think they'll pay much attention to me. I'll have to earn her trust gradually."

Sam smoothed her hand up and down his arm a few times. "Please be careful. I'm getting attached to you. I don't want to lose you now."

That was a big admission on her part. He grabbed her hand and pressed it to his lips before he pulled her close to him and planted a lustful kiss on her mouth.

"Believe me, I don't want to do anything to jeopardize our relationship...or me."

She returned his kiss, keeping her gaze locked to his. After a long moment, she sighed and looked down.

"I'm not ready to wear a collar or anything, but I am ready to be exclusive, to commit myself to you. If you get hurt, I'm going to be wrecked."

Yes! He hadn't expected her to be so open yet, but he needed to reassure her. If she felt too vulnerable, she might pull away. He placed his hand under her chin and forced her to look at him once again.

"I can't promise I won't get hurt. My job is dangerous on many levels. But I survived some of the most perilous places on Earth, and I know how to handle myself. Coming back to you is now a priority for me, so I will be very, very careful when I'm there."

"Okay, but that won't keep me from worrying about you."

She returned to eating as though the subject was closed. She expected him to come back to her, and it upped the ante for him. He would have to use all his combat experience to make sure he came out of this situation unscathed. She was surrendering to him, slowly but surely, and he needed to be there for her. She would never forgive him if he let her down. And he would never forgive himself.

Sam couldn't believe she had confessed her feelings to Mike, but she had been so frightened about his mission she hadn't been able to help herself. If she could influence his actions, make him be safer because he felt obligated to her, then it was worth it. Anyway, it was probably time she did. How long was she going to let Alex affect her relationships with men? Hadn't he done enough damage?

She was involved with a man she could trust...she knew it deep inside. Mike treated her with such care, such kindness, such attention to her needs that she had been able let go of her fears and take a chance again on a D/s relationship. She craved it, and she had denied herself the true pleasure and satisfaction of submitting to someone who could take her fears, her burdens and her insecurities and help her deal with them in a way that would bring her real happiness—something she hadn't had in a long time. Yes, she loved her work and her friends, but she also needed to love and be loved by a man she could let go with and truly be herself. Mike was that man, but if he got badly hurt or even killed, she'd never forgive him.

She chuckled to herself at that stupid thought. Of course he'd never intentionally do anything to get himself hurt. She had to accept he was in a dangerous business, and being with him was a risk she had to take. A worthwhile risk. He touched her in ways no one — not even Alex — had ever done before, slicing her open to reveal her deepest, darkest fantasies and dreams, and he wasn't put off by them. He had just the right sadistic bent to feed her particular masochism, and the sensitivity to feed her feminine soul. *A definite keeper.*

"What's so funny?" Mike's question pulled her from her thoughts.

"I just realized how silly it was of me to be annoyed at you for putting yourself in danger. I guess I have to accept the job you do and find ways to deal with it."

"Honestly, most of the jobs I get aren't that bad. But this one I have to follow through on because of Derek. I wouldn't be here for you if it wasn't for him."

"I know. I was never one for prayer, but I think I'll start."

Mike smiled at her. "Whatever works for you. I'll wrap this up as soon as I can. Unfortunately, I'm going to be working evening shifts for a while, so I won't be able to see you as much as I have been."

Sam shook her head. "I can't believe it. I finally tell you how I feel and you take off." She held her hand up as Mike opened his mouth to protest. "I know. It's not your fault. And I know you care about me. So I'll be patient. Just come back to me in one piece."

"I'll do my best."

Mike stood up to clear the dishes and Sam got up to help him. He pulled her into a tight embrace, kissing her on the forehead before letting her go. The tender act was just like him, giving her the reassurance of his touch when she needed it. What would she do if he didn't come back? As the tears welled up, she blinked furiously so Mike wouldn't see how upset she was. She grabbed the platter of leftover spaghetti and brought it to the counter, then retrieved a container to put it in. By the time Mike reached the sink with the dishes, she had collected herself enough that he didn't see her distress.

They quietly cleaned up what little there was. After they were finished, Mike turned to her. He folded her into his arms, looked down at her and asked, "Are you up for a little game? I want to imprint myself on you before I have to be away for a few days."

"What did you have in mind?"

Was that an evil glint in his eye as he answered? "A little guessing game. I pick a number between one and one thousand. You have to guess the number. For each wrong answer you give me, you get five taps with a cane."

"I'm not sure I like those odds. That's a lot of numbers to go through."

"I will help you out by telling you if the number is higher or lower than the one you guessed. You should be able to narrow it down before you can't take anymore."

She hesitated. The cane was mean. It wasn't that she didn't get off on it, but it took a long time to process the pain before she could reach subspace. Mike interrupted her thoughts.

"It won't be full-on strikes. It will be firm taps that you'll definitely feel, but I'm not going to pull back and let it rip. You should be able to deal with it. And you always have your safeword. I think you'll enjoy it."

His look of expectation persuaded her to try. His broad smile when she said 'yes' was worth it even more.

"Come with me," he said as he held out his hand. He led her into the living room and had her bend over the arm of the couch. Her feet were still able to touch the ground, so there wasn't too much pressure on her stomach—a good thing since she'd just eaten.

"Now, I'm going to write down a number, and we can begin."

"Aren't you missing a crucial toy?"

He stood in front of her with a bright green Lucite cane in his hand. "I was hoping you would say yes, so I put it in here before I made dinner. Your first guess is a freebie. So, what's your number?"

"Five hundred."

"Higher."

Okay, so in one guess she had eliminated five hundred numbers. Maybe this wouldn't be as difficult as she thought.

"Seven hundred fifty."

"Nope. Lower."

The five short taps he counted out with glee were soft but firm with just enough power to sting. The Lucite was unforgiving, so every tap bit into her before it bounced off her butt. She took a deep breath to center herself, hoping he would soothe the burn by stroking her, but he merely waited till she gave her next number.

"Seven hundred."

"Nope. Higher."

Crap! Another five short taps over the first ones right where her butt and thighs met, a very tender spot. If he kept this up it was going to become agonizing. A few more deep breaths and she ventured forth again.

"Seven hundred ten."

"Nope. Higher."

Once again the tapping hit the same sit spot, the sting increasing to the point she couldn't keep still. Kicking her feet helped her to process the pain, but Mike wasn't having it.

"Stay still or I will tie your feet to the legs of the couch."

"I'll try, but it isn't easy." She attempted to keep the whine out of her voice.

"The next time you kick, it doubles the taps."

Her voice raised in protest. "Not fair! You're changing the rules mid-game."

He bent down so he could meet her gaze. "Just clarifying them."

She bit back her snarky response, afraid he would up the ante even more.

"Number?" he coaxed.

Her brain was starting to get muddled, and she wasn't sure what the best strategy was. Go a lot higher or a little? She decided to be methodical. She'd kick herself if she skipped over the number.

"Seven hundred twenty."

"Nope. Higher."

The cheerfulness in his voice was getting annoying. He was enjoying it too much. She wouldn't admit, even to herself, that she was too.

The five taps had her kicking again. The stinging was intensifying, leaving behind a continual burn, and it was getting harder to take.

A long, dramatic sigh came from behind her. "I guess we'll have to tie those legs."

Conveniently, he had rope on the end table, and she was trussed to the couch in short order. *Thank God.* It was easier to be bound than to have to control herself.

"Five more for your punishment, and then you can guess again."

Without being able to kick, it took her longer to process the stinging fire as it lit up her ass. Her whole body tensed and she folded in closer to the arm of the couch.

"Ooooowwww! Is *that* allowed?" she shouted in exasperation.

Again his face was in front of hers. She could barely hear him as he told her, "It's allowed if it's respectful. Genuine. That was definitely not respectful. Five more."

"Fuck!"

"Five more for that. I'd compose myself, or you're going to have more punishment strikes than guessing ones."

It took all she had not to tell him to go fuck himself. Was she a masochist? Yes. But in the middle of the pain it was hard to remember she liked it. That it would lead her to a place of pleasure. And she wasn't going to win. The more she pushed him, the more he'd push back. He wouldn't let her off the hook...or allow her to top from the bottom.

Begrudgingly, she apologized for the sake of her ass. He accepted graciously but gave her ten more anyway. The only thing she had left to respond with were tears. And a long low moan of pain. As soon as he realized she was crying, he bent down to her and asked, "Are you okay? Do you want to safeword?"

She shook her head. "I can't help the crying. It's really hurting now. But I don't want to stop."

"That's my lovely girl. Courage. You'll make it. I have faith in you."

He brushed his hand down her back and over her burning butt, gently rubbing. It was the soothing relief and contact she needed to go on. Before she was ready, though, Mike stood up and repositioned himself at her side.

"All set?" he asked.

As she'd ever be. "Yes." A firm tap reminded her to add the "Sir." *Dammit! Where was I with the numbers?* She had never been that good with math. Practice in the kitchen had her able to do what she needed to multiply measurements, but otherwise her mind went numb when she needed to do any calculations. Not that this was so difficult, but she was having trouble keeping track of where she was. It might have something to do with the consequence she faced if she got it wrong.

"I can't remember the last number. Would you please help me, Sir?" she asked in her most conciliatory tone.

"Just this once. Part of the game is remembering your number. But I'll give it to you this time. Seven hundred twenty, and I said higher."

"Seven hundred thirty."

"Nope. Higher."

Tap, tap, tap, tap, tap!

"God, that hurts!" she exclaimed, hoping her expression of distress was genuine enough for him.

"It's supposed to. That's the whole point, isn't it?" He chuckled.

She was ready to punch him. But she realized she had to calm down and not let him rattle her or she'd lose track of the number and her ass couldn't afford that. And she didn't want to give him the satisfaction of punishing her again. This was a mind game as well and she didn't want to lose. She centered herself with deep breaths.

"Seven hundred forty."

"Nope. Lower."

Okay, progress. No matter what, there were no more than nine numbers left. She steeled herself for the cane.

"Relax. It will hurt more when you tense up," he counseled her.

"It won't hurt much less," she retorted.

"Fine. Have it your way."

She was ready to leave her skin by the time he delivered the last firm tap. She knew he hadn't increased the strength of the strikes, but they hurt so much more now. What had started out as eminently bearable was fast becoming too much. Was she going to make it? She didn't want to let herself...or him...down. *Think! Think!* Go down with the numbers or up? She'd kick herself if she went back to one and it was nine. *Suck it up, baby,* she admonished herself, *and be methodical. Only nine more, tops.*

"Seven hundred thirty-nine."

"Nope. Lower."

She screamed when he was done. Besides the tears, it was her only outlet for the raging inferno that was now playing out on her ass. The build-up from the tapping was such that even the slightest touch was now a serious sting. She could feel the sweat rolling down her neck and her palms were hurting from her nails digging in when she made a fist during the relentless tapping. She needed a rest, and he gave it to her, stroking her back and waiting patiently for her next number. The contact gave her the courage she needed to go on.

"Thirty-eight."

"Nope. Lower."

She screamed through all the taps. She couldn't help it anymore. She wouldn't be sitting comfortably for a while, which she guessed was his point. To remember him when he was gone. Thank goodness she stood all day in the kitchen.

"Thirty-seven."

"Nope. Lower."

If she heard the word 'nope' again, she'd kill him. She rode through the pain then mustered up her most polite tone and asked him not to use it anymore.

"I guess I can do that," he agreed. "Number?"

"Thirty-six."

"No. Lower."

She cried even before he touched her. Her frustration was growing with the pain. Should she go back to one and go up? What if it was thirty-six? *Dammit!* She was committed. She had to keep going down.

"Thirty-five?"

"Uh-uh. Lower."

By the time she made it to thirty-one, she was a screaming, crying mess, pounding on the couch pillows, angry at herself for not starting at thirty-one in the first place. Mike untied her quickly and sat down on the couch, cradling her in his arms.

"You did really well, Sam. You stuck it out. I'm impressed."

Her sniffling response was unintelligible. It was such a trite thought, but she was so cute in her distress. It made him want to comfort her in the worst way, bringing out the counterpoint to his sadism. He tightened his hold on her, hoping his strength would settle her and allow her to relax. She melted into his embrace as he felt all the tension leave her body.

"How do you feel?"

"Like jelly, like I don't have any bones left in my body."

"Is that a good thing?"

"Oh yes, Sir."

She sat back and smiled up at him. Even with her reddened eyes and wild hair curled from sweat, she was still beautiful. He could hold her like this for hours. To keep her from sitting on her tortured ass, he'd had her straddle him, resting her thighs on his and letting her ass hover between his legs. She shimmied herself closer.

"Are you sure you want to do that?" he asked. "I would think getting much closer is going to put pressure on that tender ass and upper thighs. I was trying to protect it."

"Now you try to protect it? I seem to recall you're the one who created the damage."

"So I did. And I enjoyed it immensely. It was the best fun I've had in a long time."

She looked at him askance. "Some kind of fun you like. Hurting girls till they cry."

"Hurting girls who like to cry through pain. Like you do, right?"

"You always want to make me admit it. Why?"

He grasped her arms firmly and made sure she was looking straight into his eyes before he spoke. "I will never, ever consciously do something you don't want. I want your consent before a scene and your feedback after. Always. If the pain I dispense is not the pain you like, I will be very upset. This only works if both of us are getting what we need."

"I need you to fuck me. Please, Sir."

"After all that? Really? I was going to give you time to recuperate."

"It's because of all that. Now that the pain has subsided a bit, I'm so turned on I can barely stand it." She wiggled against him and chuckled. "It seems like you are too."

"You are absolutely right, my lovely girl. Watching you suffer through my game turned me way the hell on. Nothing would please me more than to fuck you. Let's get you back over the arm of the couch. I think you'll be more comfortable that way."

She didn't hesitate. She pushed off his thighs and was over the arm in a flash. He reached into his pants pocket for a condom before he shed his clothes. He was so ready, she didn't have to ask twice. After placing the condom on his cock, he plunged into her, curling himself over her back. He could feel the heat radiating from her ass and it made him that much harder. Her answering moan of pleasure urged him on.

Reaching under her, he grasped both her nipples in his fingers and rolled them around as he slowly pumped in and out. As he accelerated his pace, he applied more pressure. She pushed herself back against him, moaning from pain or pleasure—he wasn't sure which. It didn't matter. Her cry of "Yessss!" told him that whatever it was, she loved it.

He reveled in her warmth, her tight channel squeezing around his cock till he was ready to burst. "Come for me, Sam." Her pussy contracted against him, milking him dry, sapping him of his strength. He too felt boneless, like jelly, as he rested against her still-shuddering body.

"Wow," was all she said.

"I second that wow."

He didn't want to pull out yet, needing to stay connected to her a while longer so he could store up the feeling of her sensuous heat for when he was alone in that bar without being able to see her. For the first time in his life, he didn't want to go on a mission.

She rested quietly under him, not moving, her breath evening out. His body fitted against hers so that her warmth radiated through him. It was the perfect aftermath of a scene and he didn't want it to end, but he had to get rid of the condom and he was sure that even though she wasn't complaining, lying like this with him on top of her had to be uncomfortable.

Reluctantly, he rose, pulling her up with him. She leaned back against his chest and he gave a quick pinch to her nipples, eliciting a satisfying yelp, before he helped her to sit on the couch. Her squeal reverberated against his cock, but it was too tired to respond. *Maybe later.*

By the time he came back to her side, she was stretched out on the sofa fast asleep. *And people say men tend to sleep right after sex.* In his experience, sleep was an equal-opportunity response. Picking her up, he carried her back to her bedroom. She snuggled into his chest, a broad smile on her face. Without letting her go, he crawled into bed, pressing himself against her, grateful for her submission, her closeness, her trust. Whether she knew it or not, she was his. He just had to be patient till she realized it herself.

Chapter Eight

Sam woke to a soft kiss. Opening her eyes, she looked up to find Mike bending over her, fully dressed. She wrapped her arms around his neck and pulled him down on the bed with her, laughing with him as he settled on top of her.

"Why aren't you in bed with me? It's still early."

"I love being in bed with you, pressed up against your glorious nakedness. Unfortunately, I have to get to work because I need to clear my plate to have time for my second job this evening."

As she ran her hand over his muscular back, she tried not to pout. This was important to him and she had to support his efforts, even though she hated the fact that she wouldn't see him for a while and, more importantly, that he would be in danger.

"I'm not going to tell you to be careful. I already said that. But come back to me soon. I'm going to miss you terribly."

"Especially since you're not allowed to come till I return." He waggled his eyebrows at her and grinned.

"That's totally mean! I have to worry about you and have no way to ease the tension?"

He brushed his lips against hers then whispered, "I have to give you some incentive for wanting me to return."

She ran her hands through his fair hair while looking steadily into his intense blue eyes. "I don't need incentive. Not anymore. You've wormed your way under my skin, and it will take more than a few days' absence for me to get you out of my system. When you're in the middle of whatever it is you need to be doing, remember I'm here, waiting for you to return, horny as hell."

He laughed loudly, then kissed her till she was breathless. When he extricated himself from her grasp and got out of bed, she felt bereft.

"I'll come back to you as soon as I can, my lovely girl. Know that I'll miss you every moment I'm gone and that I'll be suffering along with you, looking forward to making love to you till you scream."

He bent down for one last quick kiss and blew her another as he left the room. She curled up in a ball, more lonely than she'd ever been in her life. Until she had his strong arms around her again, she knew she wasn't going to sleep well or eat well or relax.

When her alarm rang, she reluctantly got up, despite feeling totally enervated by her loss, and got ready for work.

Rebecca was in the kitchen when she arrived, already engaged in making cookies for their upcoming event. Sam walked over to her and just stood there until Rebecca acknowledged her.

"Hey, are you all right?"

"No, and it's all your fault."

Rebecca hugged Sam, exclaiming, "I'm going to kill that son of a bitch! He promised me he wouldn't hurt you!"

Pulling out of Rebecca's embrace, Sam stroked Rebecca's arms in what she hoped was a reassuring gesture. "He hurt me only in ways I loved. It's not that. He's going away on a dangerous job, and not only am I going to miss him terribly, but I'm worried sick over it."

Rebecca brought Sam back into a hug. "You fell for him! I'm so glad. I knew he's the right man for you."

Sam nuzzled farther into Rebecca's embrace. "Okay, Becs, so you were right," she conceded. "But he just left and I'm already going crazy waiting for him to come back. I feel like I'm climbing the walls!"

"That's what your trusty Hitachi is for."

Sam whined in frustration. "He won't let me use it. I have to wait till he returns before I can come."

Rebecca laughed so hard Sam wanted to kill her. "Oh my God, Sam. He's actually got you under his control! Good for him—and you. I knew it, I knew it, I knew it!" She began to dance around the kitchen while Sam watched her with hands on her hips, throwing daggers for looks.

Rebecca danced back over to her. "Sweetie, I know it's difficult with him being away in a dangerous situation. I'm not trying to make light of that. But I'm so happy you've found someone you can trust enough to truly submit. You deserve to be happy, even in misery."

"What's making Sam happy?" Mya asked as she walked in on the tail end of the conversation.

"Not what, who," Rebecca replied.

"Sam's got a who? Really? Who is it?" Allegra chimed in, coming into the kitchen right behind Mya.

Sam rolled her eyes, threw up her hands and walked into the office to get away from the inquiring minds. She heard Rebecca tell them it was Mike, and the resultant squeals forced her to sit down with her hands over her ears. She wasn't able to hide there long. The noise in the doorway to the office demanded her attention.

Three smiling faces greeted her as her fellow chefs crowded into the office.

"We're so happy for you, Sam," Mya said. "I love Mike! And not just because he helped save my life."

"He's such a good guy," Allegra chimed in. "He's always so nice and polite to me."

"And it's time for you to have a good guy," Rebecca added.

Sam regarded the happy grins directed at her and couldn't help but smile back at them. These were her peeps, and they only wanted the best for her. She got up and walked the few short steps to allow them to hug her.

"Okay, okay," she said after only a short moment. "You've had your chance to make a fuss over this. Now we go back to normal. C'mon, we have three hundred people to feed in two days. Enough gossip, it's time for work."

"Since when can't we gossip and work at the same time?" Mya asked, her hands raised, a look of innocence on her face.

"Let me clarify—enough gossip about me. How about we hear a little about you for a while."

Mya smiled. "Not much to tell. Things are great with me and Jake. We've been playing a lot lately. And I still see the shrink once a week. I'm feeling really good."

"I'm glad," Sam said.

She gave Mya a peck on the cheek, then shooed them all out of the office. In no time the kitchen was humming with the sounds of the big Hobart mixer along with chopping, sautéing and washing of dishes. Sam breathed a sigh of relief. Here she could relax a bit, turning her attention to her work — work that she loved surrounded by women she loved.

By the time the day was over, which was almost ten at night, Sam was exhausted. When she crawled into bed, she was grateful for the taxing nature of her work. It wouldn't take long for her to fall asleep despite her worries. She wished Mike would at least call to tell her he was all right.

At that moment, a text came through.

Sweet dreams my lovely girl. Know that I am thinking of you.

Sam stretched out and lay on her back to return the text.

Glad you're all right. Thinking of you too.

She added a blowing-kiss emoji and settled into bed. Tonight she could sleep. He was safe — at least for now.

* * * *

Mike wiped down the bar, surreptitiously watching Cassie fidget while Frankie played a game of pool with two other Pagans. There were no other women in the bar, and Mike suspected Frankie was worried Cassie could be tempted by the other guys. That was a good sign. It meant they weren't so close that Cassie might not entertain the idea of leaving Frankie.

For the life of him, Mike couldn't figure out what Cassie saw in Frankie. He was loud, uncouth and not particularly handsome. Cassie had been raised in a comfortable middle-class home with loving parents who gave her lots of attention. Why did she feel the need to abandon her parents to go off with this piece of shit? It left him shaking his head in disbelief.

But he had to believe it. Here she was sitting in this bar, watching Frankie play and being careful not to look any other man in the eyes. He suspected Frankie was so jealous that he must jump down her throat if he thought she was flirting with anyone else. Which gave him a bit of an idea. What if Frankie became jealous of him?

He walked over to Cassie slowly, so as not to disrupt the game and call attention to himself.

"Hi," he said as he approached.

Cassie regarded him with surprise. She furtively looked over to see if Frankie noticed he was there, and when she was sure he was playing and not paying the slightest attention to her, she turned and said, "Hi."

"Do you need a drink?"

She shook her head. "Frankie doesn't like me to drink. He says it makes me stupid."

"I can't believe that," Mike answered.

"He's right," she countered. "I don't hold my liquor very well. Thanks anyway. And I shouldn't be talking to you, so I'd appreciate it if you'd go back behind the bar."

"Of course," Mike answered, although he didn't move. "But it's hard to watch a lovely young woman like yourself sit all alone."

A veil of red rose over her face. "I'm not lovely," she objected. "But Frankie likes me anyway. So, I'm good here." She nodded to confirm and smiled at Frankie as he glanced at her for a moment. But Frankie took one look at Mike and growled. The smile faded from Cassie's face.

"Please, leave me alone!" she demanded, sotto voce so Frankie wouldn't hear. "I'm going to get in trouble."

"I wouldn't want that," Mike said. This time he did move, not ready for things to come to a head quite yet. She didn't trust him, and he needed time to change that.

Back behind the bar, Mike studied the situation. Frankie wasn't paying her that much attention and she was left to sit all by herself. Was he that good a fuck that she would leave her whole world behind for this loser? It couldn't be the only reason. He would need to work on her to find that out. But even though they hung out at the bar on a regular basis, it was going to be hard to get close to her under Frankie's watchful eye.

Mike went about his business, serving customers, commenting now and again to try to insinuate himself into the bar community enough that they might talk to him a little and share some much-needed information. No one bit. It was a tight-knit group and outsiders were not welcome. He'd have to rely solely on his powers of observation.

Once Frankie's game was finished, he walked over and took possession of Cassie. It was the only way Mike could describe it. Frankie leaned against a table and pulled Cassie into his embrace, sticking his hand in her back pocket, effectively trapping her in his clutches. He plundered her mouth with such intensity that the only thing keeping her upright was his arm around her. Mike was sure he saw a slight hesitation, a tensing on Cassie's part, before she put her arms around Frankie and surrendered to him.

Maybe she was just uncomfortable with PDAs. But maybe it was something more, something he could use. He'd have to be patient. It was just day one, and he couldn't expect to be successful so soon. *Fuck!* This was going to be a long haul.

Frankie kept a hold on Cassie the rest of the time they were there. He placed her on his lap while he drank far too many beers, shouting and making a spectacle of himself. The whole time Cassie remained quiet, sitting demurely, only moving to avoid a wayward arm as Frankie punctuated his words with jabs of his fingers. His Pagan brothers seemed to put up with his taunts and gave back in kind. It was the classic dysfunctional family, creating their closeness through insults and criticism.

By the time his shift was over, Mike had heard enough bullshit to last a long time. Not that he wasn't used to crude language and foul banter. He'd been in the military. But this reached a level of crudeness even he found offensive, and it only intensified his bewilderment as to what Cassie was doing in the midst of this filth.

His answer would have to wait. After he closed down the bar and locked up, he trudged to his truck, realizing he hadn't been so worn out in a while. It wasn't just physical. The stench of the Pagans had infiltrated his being, and it was all he could do to keep the nausea at bay. And he was worried about Derek's daughter. He hoped she had driven home, because Frankie had been in no condition to do it himself.

His own home was a welcome sight, and after quickly shedding his clothes he texted Sam that he was home safe. He crawled into bed, acutely aware of the emptiness caused by her absence. *Hmmm,* he thought as he drifted to sleep, *maybe she could come here to sleep so that I can curl up beside her warm delicious body when I get home.*

* * * *

Two days of nonstop cooking kept Sam from thinking too much about Mike. Not that she didn't have an insistent ache inside needing to be filled. Or that she couldn't wait to hear his voice again, telling her what to do, demanding that she obey. More than once, one of her fellow chefs had to admonish her not to take her anxiety out on them or the servers at the party. Three hundred people demanded constant vigilance in the kitchen to ensure everything went smoothly, that nothing burned or got out of the kitchen at the wrong temperature, and that all the garnishes got on the proper plates.

Mike had sent short messages telling her he was thinking of her, but they hadn't had a real conversation in days. Neither of them had the time.

After the event was over, while Sam was driving the van back to the kitchen, depression came crashing in on her. Exhaustion, loneliness, fear and unfulfilled sexual desire all preyed on her until tears began to fall without warning. A small sniffle caught Rebecca's attention.

"Pull over, I'm driving," Rebecca demanded.

"I'm okay. I can drive," Sam argued.

"No you're not, and I'm not risking my life because you're too stubborn to admit you're hurting."

Rebecca was right, as always. She couldn't afford to put her best friend in jeopardy, and she certainly wanted to be around when Mike finished his job. She pulled over and exited the van, going around the front while Rebecca slid into the driver's seat. When she was settled in the passenger seat, Rebecca started up again.

"The event went well tonight. Mrs. Russo said she was so happy she would definitely recommend us to her friends."

"Terrific," Sam replied without much enthusiasm, swiping the sleeve of her chef coat across her cheeks to wipe away her tears.

"It is terrific. We made a lot of money on this account, and if we can do more of them, we'll be able to expand the way we want to."

"You're right, Becs. But I can't wrap my head around it right now. I wish Mike would call to let me know he's okay."

Rebecca leaned over and patted Sam's thigh. "He's fine. He's texted you, right? He just doesn't have the time to call."

Sam let out a frustrated sigh. "I guess. But I'd like to have some kind of contact with him."

"I know. Can you call him?"

"I don't feel comfortable doing that. I don't want to interrupt him or do anything that might put him in jeopardy. I have no idea what he's up against, and that's what's driving me crazy!"

Sam's voice had risen almost an octave by the time she was finished. Rebecca shot her a distressed look.

"I don't think I've ever seen you so upset. Why don't you come stay with me and Ethan tonight? I don't think you should go home alone when you're so tired. It diminishes your coping skills."

"I appreciate the offer, but I think I prefer to go home. But thanks, Becs. If I change my mind, I'll let you know."

"You know you're always welcome with us."

"Of course. And it means a lot to me. I'm closer to you than my own family."

"We are family. At least I think we are."

Sam gave Rebecca a grateful smile. She knew she was lucky to have so many people in her corner. At the moment, though, it wasn't enough to lighten her mood.

At the kitchen, they all unloaded the vans of the empty coolers and put all the other catering tools away. Sam said goodbye and drove home in silence, not even bothering to put on music. An empty house further accentuated her mood and she plopped herself into a chair and put her feet up on an ottoman, too tired and distraught to get undressed and go to bed. She passed out from fatigue and tumbled into a night of bad dreams.

* * * *

Sunday morning, Mike woke to such a need for Sam it took him no time to shower, dress and grab his toy bag. She didn't have a party today, and although she must have come home late from the event last night, he couldn't wait any longer to get his hands on her. She could sleep when he went to the bar.

It took her a few minutes to open the door after he pounded on it to wake her up. She was still in her chef coat and pants, her hair disheveled and mascara smeared under her eyes. Her eyes widened in disbelief when she saw him, and with a cry of relief she crumbled into his waiting arms.

"Thank god! I've been so worried."

Holding her tight, he stroked her back. "I'm fine. That's what the texts were for, my lovely girl. So you wouldn't worry."

"I can't help it. Something could always happen a minute after your last text."

"How about you let me in and we can discuss my solution to the problem."

He didn't wait for her to step aside. He lifted her in his arms and crossed the threshold, kicking the door closed behind him. Dropping his bag by the door, he carried her as far as the couch, sat down with her on his lap and kissed her hard, his delight at seeing her combined with his hunger compelling him to devour her. She melted into him, opening up in sublime surrender.

He needed her naked. To feel her flesh against his flesh. To get as close as humanly possible. He started unbuttoning her chef coat.

"Wait. I'm still sweaty from last night. I'll go shower."

"Can't wait. Help me get these clothes off. Now!"

She jumped up and shed her pants and panties in one motion. He let her finish with the chef coat while he undressed himself. Once naked, he pulled her toward him, pressing against her head to toe. It wasn't enough.

Maintaining his hold, he guided her onto the couch, his need to be inside her so great he felt like he might explode. Separating from her only long enough to grab a condom from his pocket and put it on, he lay down over her.

"Open for me. I can't wait one second longer to have you," he growled.

She didn't hesitate, bringing up her knees and planting her feet on either side of his hips, fully exposing herself. Reaching down to massage her clit, he felt the telltale wetness he'd hoped for. She was as ready for him as he was for her.

"Hold on, baby. This will be quick and rough."

At her gasped, "Yes!" he plunged inside her warm depths, the walls of her pussy clutching him with the same desperation he felt. As he pounded her relentlessly, her continued cries of "Yes! Yes! Yes!" spurred him on until they both screamed out their release and collapsed into each other.

They lay there for a few moments trying to catch their breath, each panting like a dog on a hot summer day. Sam started to laugh.

"What?" he asked.

"I needed that as much as you did. So, so good."

He stroked her hair and down her cheek. "Yes. So, so good. Now that I've assuaged my need a bit, let's get you in the shower."

"I knew I smelled bad!" she cried with a look of horror.

"Not possible. I love how you smell even after a day of work. It's all you, not masked by soap or perfumes. It appeals to my primal instinct. And you smell as delicious after a sweaty session of sex as you do right after a shower. I just think you'll feel better once you you're clean."

She didn't look like she believed him. But after he grabbed his pants, which housed his supply of condoms, she allowed him to pull her up and lead her to the bathroom. He discarded the condom he had on, grabbed another from his pocket and followed her into a steaming shower. As the water sluiced down her curves, he felt himself once again rise to the occasion. But this time he wanted to savor the experience.

He put the condom on the shelf, then grabbed the bottle of shower gel and poured the gelatinous liquid into his hands.

"I have a loofah to use with that. It suds better," she informed him.

"I don't care. I want to feel your skin as I wash you."

Rubbing his hands together, he built up a small bit of lather. Starting at her breasts, he massaged the liquid onto her skin, paying special attention to the beautiful dark pink peaks that were now standing at attention. Her deep-throated, answering moan spurred him on. He pinched each nipple between his fingers, causing her to bend her knees and tremble.

"More of that and I'll need to come, Sir."

"I think I'll have you wait for the next one, greedy girl. I want to take my time exploring this body, which I missed so much in the past few days."

"A body that has been denied release, making it very sensitive to stimuli."

He palmed both breasts and pulled her against him. She'd feel his erection against her back, so she'd know he was as turned on as she was.

"A body that will submit to my demands. A body that will take what I give. A body that will allow me to pleasure it in my own time."

He squeezed her nipples again, hard, and her squealed "Yes, Sir" made him laugh in delight. Releasing his hold, he slowly smoothed his hands down her stomach until he reached her mound. She opened her legs to grant him access. To throw her off balance, he started to wash her back next.

"Are you kidding me?" she whined.

"What did I just tell you? Patience and you get what you need. Complain and you get what you don't want."

Her shoulders slumped, but she didn't say any more. He meticulously washed every inch of her back before he moved around her waist and sought the place where she most desired attention. Her appreciative sigh elicited a chuckle.

"You're making fun of me," she accused.

"Never. I love your desire, your passion, your need. It corresponds to my own."

He swiped a finger through wetness he knew wasn't caused by the shower. Circling her clit, he massaged her until she cried out, "Please, Sir, I can't hold back much longer."

"I don't think I can either," he said as he opened the condom packet and stretched the condom on his rigid cock. Positioning her so she was holding on to the towel bar, he entered her from behind. She backed up and pushed until he was fully inside.

"I was going to take my time this go-around," he admonished.

"Sorry, Sir, I couldn't wait."

"You will stay still now, and don't move a muscle or I will pull out for good. You'll finish me off with your mouth and I won't allow you to come."

Her whole body tensed in attention.

"Relax and let's ride this feeling together."

"Yes, Sir," she said, the contrition evident in her voice. Her desperation in the face of his absence had compelled her to lose control, and he understood it. But he had to take back the reins for both their sakes. Their dynamic worked best when he was in charge.

He took his time, as he'd promised. Slow, long, deliberate strokes propelled them both closer and closer to the brink of orgasm without pushing them over. She trembled in his arms as her pussy fluttered around him, clutching at him each time he entered as though she were trying to prevent him from leaving again. The incredible friction had all his feeling centered in his dick, demanding release but not wanting to quite let go because the ride felt so good. After a while, though, even he couldn't take it anymore. Commanding her to "Come with me!", he exploded inside her trembling depths, desperately holding on to keep them both upright.

He was everything she needed, hoped for, desired but never thought she could have. Lost in a maelstrom of emotion, Sam relied on Mike to hold her up — and hold her together. He supported her until she stopped trembling and was able to stand up straight. Then he poured out more shower gel and went back to washing her, starting with her pussy.

He was gentle, respecting her sensitivity in the wake of two orgasms in a short time. She loved him for it, his perception of her needs and his taking care of them, creating a cocoon around her where she could feel totally safe. It was a feeling she treasured, one she didn't want to lose.

By the time he was finished washing her feet, she felt cherished, a sub of true worth to the Dom who wanted to care for her as much as play with her. She'd told him she couldn't commit long-term, but she was fast becoming ready to do so.

"May I wash you, Sir? You've done such a wonderful job for me, I feel I should reciprocate."

"As much as I would love that, I think we should both have a rest, something that won't happen if you wash me. You should get out and dry off, but don't get dressed. I'll be quick and meet you in the kitchen. I haven't had breakfast and I know you haven't either."

"Of course. I'll get it started."

She got out, dried off and brushed the tangles from her hair before going to make breakfast. The coffee was ready by the time he arrived, looking shiny with his glistening wet hair and his skin ruddy from the hot steam in the shower. He was wearing his jeans but hadn't put his shirt or shoes back on, so she could admire his well-cut abs.

"Like what you see?" he asked, his blue eyes dancing with mirth.

"Every last bit," she answered, unabashed at her admiration of his impressive physique.

"Good. I like that I can turn you on with my physical charms. It's one more tool in my arsenal to get you to commit to me."

She stopped chopping onions for the omelet she was making, walked up to him and pressed against his imposing frame. "Your physical charms were the first thing that turned me on about you. That wasn't nearly enough for me to commit. It's your strength of character, your caring as a Dom, your playfulness, your incredibly magic hands that have me on the verge of a commitment."

He squeezed her. "Wow. You like me for my brains as well as my brawn. I'm so happy!"

She giggled into his chest. "Yes, Sir, you are the full package, and I'm not just talking about what's between your legs."

His joyful laugh created a contented warmth throughout her body. They stood leaning against each other for a while, enjoying the rapport they were now willing to admit to. Only a rumbling from Mike's stomach compelled her to let go and resume cooking.

"Breakfast will be ready soon. Coffee is finished dripping, so if you want to help yourself, the cups are above the coffeemaker."

"I'm famished. I've worked up quite an appetite. You took a lot out of me."

"To make up for it, I'm preparing you a sumptuous breakfast so you can regain your strength. I'm going to need at least one more fuck before you go to work."

He winked at her. "Don't you worry, greedy girl. I'll be sure you're well satisfied before I leave. Be careful what you wish for."

"You don't scare me."

He got serious immediately, his eyes blazing with emotion. "I sincerely hope not. Excited anticipation yes, but real fear never. I promise to care for you always."

Placing her knife on the counter, she broke eye contact, unable to keep the intense connection. She took a deep breath to center herself before she looked back at him.

"I trust you, Mike. Implicitly. Never doubt that. You've given me more in a few weeks than I've had in my whole life..." She needed another deep breath to continue without tears. "...and I'm so grateful to you."

He embraced her before she finished speaking. She hugged him as tightly as he hugged her. While she tried to keep from crying, he only made it worse by kissing her on top of her head, then down her face till he pressed his lips against the pulse point in her neck. Tenderness, caring and...dare she think it?...love flowed from him. Overwhelmed, she broke, crying into his neck.

"Hey, the last thing I want to do is make you cry," he said softly, pulling back to force her to look at him. "I want to make you happy."

She rolled her eyes through her tears. "Boy, you don't know women as much as I thought you did. We always cry when we're overwhelmed with happiness."

"Well then, cry me a river, my lovely girl. Just lean on me and let go. I'm here for you."

His statement unleashed another torrent of tears, and she collapsed into his embrace just as he instructed. By the time she came to her senses, she was wrung out. She huffed a laugh.

"I don't think anyone has made me cry as much as you have."

"I'm sorry," he said with such sincerity she had to hug him again.

"It's nothing to be sorry about. You've tapped into emotions I buried long ago. It's nice to feel again."

He leaned down to brush his lips against hers, then planted a gentle kiss. "Feeling better?"

She nodded.

"Then do you think you could finish making breakfast? You know the way to a man's heart is through his stomach, right?"

She was still smiling when she put the omelets on the table. Bacon, cheese, mushrooms, peppers and onions spilled out of the ends of the rolled-up delicacies, the fragrant aroma causing Mike to breathe deeply and smile.

"This is fantastic! What a way to start the day."

Sam eyed him coyly. "Not exactly the start of the day. *That* was fantastic!"

"You have a point. But this looks and smells incredible. I can't wait to dig in."

"Please do before it gets cold."

Sam sat back and watched Mike eat with zest until he looked up and caught her observing him. "You should eat before yours gets cold as well," he admonished.

She nodded, starting in on her own food even as she relished his enjoyment. She could get used to doing this every morning.

After they finished breakfast, Mike loaded the dishwasher while she washed the skillet, knife and cutting board. Then he led her into the living room, having her sit on an easy chair while he faced her on the ottoman, taking her hands in his, massaging her thumb with his own. His somber expression made her nervous.

"You said you're worried when you can't be with me. I have an idea about how to fix that...not totally, because you can't come with me to the bar...but at least so we can see each other every day. I want you to come stay in my house until this is over. That way I can crawl in next to you each night when I come home."

He hesitated, giving her time to mull it over. She liked the idea. It would be so nice to sleep with him, to be close to him all night even if she couldn't spend any more time with him than that. *Yup, it would work.*

"I'd love to. I've missed you so much these past few days, more than I imagined I possibly could. I wouldn't worry so much if I could touch you at least once a day...I think. When you're at that bar, it's hard for me not to be frantic with worry."

His smile was ear to ear.

"Yes! I was hoping you'd say yes. You can pack up some things and come over today before I leave for work."

"If you could leave me a key, I'd rather come over later. It's my one day I can get things done before I start a new event. You won't be there till late anyway, and I'll need my car there in the morning. I also want to shop for food. Am I wrong in assuming you don't have much for breakfast or a late dinner?"

"No, you wouldn't be wrong. I'd love you to be there before I leave tonight, but I understand. Let me give you the key right now so we don't forget. I intend to keep you preoccupied with other things for the rest of the time I'm here."

He reached into his pocket for his keys. Detaching one from his keychain, he handed it to her. No sooner did she place it on the table next to her than Mike pulled her into his arms.

"Do you want to go back into the bedroom and have a semi-quickie or would you like a bit of bondage to go with your sex?"

"I think I definitely have time for bondage."

"Terrific. Bring me the pink rope in my bag."

She dug out the rope and eagerly brought it to him. She loved when he tied her in his web of rope, capturing her mind as well as her body.

He had her in a rope corset with her breasts fully wrapped in a matter of minutes. Then he instructed her to lie back over the coffee table, to which he bound her hands and feet. It wasn't as comfortable as being on a spanking bench, but he put a pillow under her head and she was comfortable enough to bear whatever he had in mind.

It was the dragontail. Her favorite. Instead of wielding it fully, he folded it in half and began to swat her breasts, which were standing up at attention in their wrappings. *Clever man.* He only brushed her nipples with the whip, which was way more painful than if he'd hit her full breast. She closed her eyes and settled against the pain, absorbing it, embracing it, letting it flow through her as it transformed into extreme pleasure centered in her core.

"Mmmmmm."

"That's it, my beautiful girl. Enjoy. Let go."

She did, letting go of all the worry and loneliness of the past few days. Just as she was drifting off to subspace, the sharp bite of the whip on her clit caught her attention, rousing her out of her almost stupor. Her eyes flew open to see the evil smile on Mike's face.

"Just wanted to be sure you knew I was still here."

"Just because I reach subspace doesn't mean I forget about you."

He flicked the tip of the dragontail against her clit again, the pain causing her hips to rise up what little they could under the circumstances.

"Truth be told, I did it 'cause I wanted to."

Again the sting of the whip graced her tender flesh.

"If you don't want me to come, you'll have to stop that," she warned.

"Who says I don't want you to come? I want to pleasure you as much as I can. Come for me," he said as he flicked the whip again.

The resulting pain sent her over, her whole body straining against her bonds as she trembled her release. Mike dropped to his knees and sucked her clit hard, prolonging the orgasm. By the time she came down, she was soaked in sweat and every muscle in her body ached with fatigue.

Mike quickly undid the bonds, sat her up and held her for a few minutes, stroking her arms and kissing her neck. Than he sat back on his heels and regarded her closely.

"Are you ready to stand?"

"I think so."

He helped her rise and made sure she was steady on her feet before he let go.

"Now we can go to the bedroom for a semi-quickie."

She laughed and nodded, allowing him to lead her by the hand to her bedroom. She was glad he hadn't removed the rope corset when he released her, keeping her in her submissive headspace.

"Hands and knees," he instructed as soon as they neared the bed. By the time she had attained her position he had rolled on a condom.

"Ready for me?"

"I'm always ready for you."

"Not true, but I love to hear it anyway."

His cock was buried to the hilt before he finished the sentence. She squeezed tightly against him, relishing his answering groan.

"You're going to kill me!"

"And you'll die happy."

"You got that right!" he cried as she squeezed him again on a return stroke.

By the time they both came, she was wrung out. She wasn't sure she'd get much done before she left for Mike's house. But it was okay. Her laundry and errands could wait. Being in Mike's arms could not. She held him tight, not wanting to let go, not wanting him to go out again in the face of danger. Where he could get hurt. Or killed.

As he began to extricate himself from her arms, she gripped him even tighter.

"Hey, I'll see you tonight. It will be okay."

"Maybe. I won't be relaxed again till you crawl in bed next to me."

He kissed her, a sweet kiss she assumed he meant to reassure rather than arouse, a kiss meant to take her mind off her worries. It didn't work, but she wouldn't belabor the point. She didn't want to be an added burden. He was dealing with enough already.

She followed him to the door after he dressed. She remained naked as much to reinforce her submission for herself as to please him. It was so hard to let him go. After one last kiss, she watched him from the window until his car was out of sight. She had a few more hours of peace before he went to the bar. She should push herself to get stuff done. Maybe it would also help take her attention off him. But in her heart she knew that no matter how much laundry or how many errands she completed, he would be ever-present in her mind.

Chapter Nine

Mike walked into the bar and immediately knew something was up. The place was abuzz with intense conversation around many of the tables. Near the pool table, Frankie was arguing with three other Pagans, obviously quite upset. Cassie was nowhere to be seen.

It was time to keep his mouth shut and his ears open. It didn't take him long to discern that the Pagans' turf had been invaded the night before and another gang had stolen a large cache of drugs from them. Some of the Pagans wanted to go get it back, while others were reluctant to go up against their rivals, who had way more members and were in a much more protected situation than theirs. Clearly, Frankie hadn't done his due diligence in setting up security for their drug supply. Things had been getting sloppy in the organization, and recriminations were flying throughout the room.

Mike was definitely concerned about this turn of events. Frankie's frustration could be turned on Cassie.

Where the hell was she, anyway? How was he going to keep her safe if he didn't know where she was?

Mike took a turn around the bar, picking up empty glasses and trying to pick up more information. As he skirted the pool table, he heard Frankie warn his cohorts that if they didn't help him get their stuff back, he was going to leave and go back to Maryland for good.

Fuck! Mike couldn't let that happen. Or at least he couldn't let Frankie take Cassie out of the state where he wouldn't be able to help her.

Much to his relief, Cassie walked into the bar with six other women who were obviously attached to the gang. Mike wasn't sure if the fact that she was being given more freedom was due to Frankie's preoccupation with his problems or because Cassie was proving to be more solid in Frankie's eyes. He hoped it was the former. The more she bonded with Frankie, the harder it was going to be to get her away from him.

The women with Cassie formed a phalanx around her, making it difficult for anyone to get near her. Had they been charged with keeping an eye on her, making sure she didn't get away? It had more of a look of menace than of congeniality. Cassie wasn't talking to any of them, and she was looking furtively around the room. Relief crossed her face the minute she spied Frankie, but it turned to distress when she realized how upset he was.

Something didn't add up. Cassie tried to extricate herself from the group to go to Frankie, but a rough-looking, heavily tattooed woman grabbed her by the arm and snarled at her. She nodded to a chair and Cassie obediently sat down.

Double fuck! Clearly there was a turf war going on inside the Pagan group itself, and Cassie was being used as a hostage to get Frankie under control. Mike walked up to the women.

"Ladies, can I get you anything?"

Some of them ordered drinks. Cassie remained silent. Mike addressed her directly, hoping to provide her with someone she might rely on.

"Cassie, would you like anything?"

Her eyes shot up to him in surprise, then a smile crossed her face as she recognized him.

"Yea, thanks. I think I'll have a Coke."

The other women laughed at her order, but Mike nodded. "Coming right up."

He left the women and made his way back to the bar. The situation had come to a head in a way that was far more volatile than he had anticipated. He wasn't only dealing with Frankie now. Cassie was being used as a bargaining chip against Frankie, which put Mike in the crosshairs of the other Pagans as well as Frankie himself if he made a move to help her.

He had to figure this out. He wasn't dealing with a very sophisticated crew. This wasn't a Mafia organization—it was more like the Bad News Bears of crime. That was a problem because they could do something stupid. And they outnumbered him. But if he could divert their attention, he might be able to get to Cassie without incident.

He brought the drinks around the room. Unfortunately it was predominantly a beer-drinking crowd, so he couldn't overload them with booze. He kept circling the bar so that the minute someone needed another drink, he was there to bring it to them. It took a few hours, but most of the patrons achieved a lethargic buzz. The conversations had calmed, but Mike knew any perceived slight could set them off. It was a delicate balance.

The rapt attention that had been paid to Cassie when the women arrived was dissipating. Some of them had gone to sit with their boyfriends. A few were engaged in their own conversation and weren't paying that much attention to Cassie. Frankie was still trying to convince his lieutenants to back him up.

Mike's moment of opportunity came when Cassie went to go to the ladies' room. He had hoped that pumping her with liquid would have an effect and eventually it did. She was dutifully shadowed by only one of her sentinels. *Yes!*

Once Cassie and her guard were inside the bathroom, Mike followed them back and went into the stockroom. He came out with a case of beer and looked around. No one else was near. After placing the case on the floor by the bathroom, he pulled out a gag and rope from the box—items he had hidden in the stockroom days before.

The door to the ladies' room wasn't lockable. He entered quickly but stealthily. Cassie was still in a stall, and her guard was standing with her back to the door, watching the stall Cassie was in. She never saw Mike coming.

He grabbed her from behind, pinning her arms to her sides while he shoved the ball gag into her surprised open mouth. He then pulled her arms behind her as he kicked her feet out from under her and brought her to the ground on her belly. In no time he had her in a hogtie with the gag secured around her head.

"If you move a muscle, I'll knife you," he warned.

Cassie emerged from the stall just as he finished. Her shocked expression forced him to grab her and put his hand over her mouth.

"Please be quiet, Cassie, and don't scream. I'm not going to hurt you. Your father sent me to help you. I need to get you out of here. I know you're being held hostage, and Frankie may not be able to protect you. Do you understand what I'm saying?"

She slumped against him and nodded. He didn't remove his hand, but he lessened his hold on her.

"I want you leave with me out the back door. You can talk to Frankie later, when you escape. Will you go with me?"

Again she nodded. This time he let her go, and thankfully she didn't scream. He opened the door and scanned the hall. No one was looking for them yet, but it wouldn't take long before they did. He grabbed her hand and led her down the hallway and out the back to his waiting car. He got them both in and started up just as two Pagans came flying through the door. Mike took off as the guys fired a hail of bullets at his car. They shattered the windshield, and even though he ducked, pulling Cassie with him, he felt the telltale sting of a bullet as he careened down the alley and out onto the street.

He didn't stop, hurtling down the street, hoping that some cop would stop them for speeding. Unfortunately, this part of town wasn't crawling with law enforcement, and it wasn't long before the noise of motorcycles was behind them. Praying he could hold on long enough to hit the highway, Mike floored the gas pedal and surged ahead.

"Call nine-one-one," he shouted to Cassie. "Tell them we're on Route 21 in Passaic and we're being chased by Pagans."

Cassie called while Mike steered onto the entrance to 21 and took off. There wasn't too much traffic, which made it easy for him to drive fast. It also made it easier for the Pagans to follow.

Finally, the sound of sirens pierced the night. Mike didn't slow, afraid the Pagans would try to shoot at him again before the cops got there. Fortunately, he was soon surrounded by flashing lights, and he made his way to the side of the road. He put the car in park and leaned back against the seat, overcome with nausea. The last thing he heard was Cassie's scream.

* * * *

Sam was frantic. It was after four a.m. and Mike still hadn't come home. Something terrible had happened. She'd known it the minute she'd woken a half hour before and Mike wasn't in bed. The Towne Tavern closed at one. Even if it took him a bit longer to clean up and shut down, he should have been home by now. She had called his phone every few minutes to no avail.

"Okay, calm down and think," she told herself. "Where are the nearest hospitals?"

She googled hospitals on her phone and called the first one on her list. And hit a roadblock immediately. No one would give her information since she wasn't next of kin.

Panic threatened to engulf her. *Where is he? Is he dead?* Desperation compelled her to call Rebecca.

"Yes?" came the sleepy voice over the phone.

Unable to stay calm, she cried, "Mike isn't home yet. Something terrible's happened. I don't know what to do!"

"Okay, sweetie. Ethan and I will be right over!" Rebecca told her, a source of calm in her hysteria.

Sam didn't even say goodbye before she hung up. She sank into the sofa and dissolved into tears. Rebecca and Ethan could be the sane ones. She didn't have it in her to do it anymore.

Her phone rang while she was waiting. *Mike! Thank god!*

"Where are you?" she demanded as soon as she answered. "I've been worried sick!"

It took a moment to register that the voice on the other end of the line wasn't Mike's.

"Sam? My name is Cassie. I'm calling because Mike's been hurt."

"Where is he? Is he okay?"

There was a pause. Sam rose from the couch to grab her coat. "Where is he?"

"He's at St. Mary's in Passaic. He's going to be okay. He got shot, but it isn't life-threatening."

"I'll be there right away."

Again she hung up without saying goodbye. It occurred to her that she should put some clothes on. As she went to the bedroom to dress, she called Rebecca.

"He's at St. Mary's," she told her as soon as she answered. "I'll meet you there." It would be faster than waiting for them to get to her.

"No," Rebecca told her. "We're on our way and I don't want you driving in your state of mind. Wait for us, please!"

"Okay," Sam conceded. She wasn't in any condition to drive. Her hands were shaking as she took off her robe and put on clothes. By the time she dressed, Rebecca and Ethan were at the door.

The ride to the hospital was endless. She had to see Mike, to touch him, to feel his warmth. She wouldn't be able to breathe properly until she could see for herself that he was all right.

They were directed to the waiting room when they arrived. Mike was heavily sedated and they couldn't see him. Entering the filled waiting room, Sam called out for Cassie. The slight, pale girl in the back with blood on her shirt raised her hand. Sam rushed over and demanded answers before she even sat down.

"What happened?"

As the story slowly unfolded, it dawned on Sam that Mike had been minimizing his danger to her. When she got her hands on him, she'd kill him. After she held him in her arms.

It was Rebecca who had the presence of mind to ask Cassie how she was doing.

"I'm overwhelmed. And so sorry Mike got hurt because of my relationship with Frankie."

"I'm glad you're okay, but we're all a little mystified as to why you were with him," Sam said.

Rebecca put her arms around Cassie. "We don't have to talk about that now," she said, throwing a disapproving look in Sam's direction.

"It's okay," Cassie answered. "I flunked out of college. I was ashamed and felt like such a failure. My father wanted me to go to community college, but I wasn't ready. I was working in a pizza place, where Frankie came in every day. He was so nice to me in the beginning. He made me feel smart and wanted. I wasn't thinking about how crazy the whole situation was. I let him sweep me off my feet, and once he had me, he wouldn't let me even think about leaving. I was too frightened and embarrassed to call my dad, so I stayed with him."

Rebecca hugged her tightly. "You're lucky your dad wouldn't let you go. It could have been really bad for you."

Cassie started cry. "If it wasn't for Mike I could have been killed. I'll always be grateful to him for saving me."

"And you won't be stupid enough to get mixed up with guys like Frankie again." The words came out of Sam's mouth without thought.

Rebecca's exasperation with her was evident as she continued to hug Cassie. "I'm sure you learned your lesson, right?" Rebecca cooed at her. Cassie nodded through her tears.

"Sorry," Sam mumbled, guilty at heaping scorn on the woman who had helped her find Mike. She should be more compassionate. Hadn't she been controlled by someone who hadn't had her best interests at heart? How could she look down on Cassie for doing the same thing?

At that moment, Ethan came up to them.

"Where were you?" Rebecca asked him.

"I was using my powers of persuasion to try to get some information about Mike."

"So, what did you find out?"

"Not much more than you. This patient confidentiality stuff is pretty impenetrable. I called Jake. He's on his way over. He has Mike's power of attorney."

"I'm going to jump out of my skin before he gets here!" Sam complained as Ethan sat down next to her.

"He should be here soon," he said, taking her hand in his and squeezing it gently. His encouraging smile was sweet.

"You've got a good one, Rebecca," she said, squeezing Ethan back.

"I know. So do you," Rebecca said. "When he comes to, I hope you let him know that."

"Believe me, I already have," Sam said in barely a whisper.

What would she do if Mike didn't recover the way they said he would? If some complication set in and he didn't make it? No, she couldn't think that way. She had to be strong for him. To only allow positive vibes in his direction. She closed her eyes, settled back against the uncomfortable chair and forced herself to be upbeat, to plan what she would do to make him feel special when he came home.

Jake's arrival pulled her from her thoughts, which had veered in a very raunchy direction. Red-faced, she looked up at her friends, who were listening to Jake's explanation of Mike's condition. Rebecca winked at her, and Sam knew she'd figured out what Sam had been dreaming about.

Jake's news was reassuring. Mike would stay in the hospital till tomorrow so they could make sure he was stable. St. Mary's had a well-regarded wound center. Fortunately, the bullet had missed the bone. After he was discharged, a visiting nurse would be assigned to change the dressing, and he needed to see the doctor in a week.

"I don't think it's good for Mike to stay alone," Rebecca observed. "Maybe you can hire someone to stay with him."

"That won't be necessary. I moved in with him yesterday."

Rebecca's mouth dropped open. "And you didn't tell me?"

"I didn't have a chance! We just decided on it. I would have told you tomorrow in the kitchen."

The look of joy from Rebecca was nauseating. Sam held up her hand. "Don't say anything! I'll discuss it with you later. Now we need to concentrate on Mike."

Rebecca didn't stop smiling, but she nodded. The men stared at the walls as though they were oblivious to what the women were discussing. Jake turned to Cassie.

"Are you Derek's daughter?"

She nodded.

"Have you told your father where you are?"

This time she shook her head, a flush of embarrassment covering her face.

"Do you want to call him or should I?"

"Please, sir, I'd appreciate it if you did it." She gave Jake the number and he walked outside to make the call.

Sam paced, unable to sit still any longer. The minute Jake returned, she accosted him. "When can I see him?"

"He'll be out for a while. You should go home and come back around eleven tomorrow. They'll discharge him by then."

"I'm not leaving. If anything happens, I want to be here. I need to be here when he wakes up." A sob escaped her lips.

Jake pulled Sam into his arms. "Okay. Okay," he said, gently patting her on the back. "I'll stay here with you."

"Thanks. At least you can get updates on how he's doing." She turned to Rebecca and Ethan. "There's no reason for you guys to hang around. You both have to be at work tomorrow." Rebecca and Ethan rose. They came over and kissed her. "You two are the best. Thanks for picking me up."

"You know you can always count on us. If you need anything, call me," Rebecca said.

Sam nodded. "I will."

Another round of kisses and Rebecca and Ethan left. Sam went to sit next to Jake, who was telling Cassie that her father was on his way and reassuring her that he wasn't mad. Cassie didn't look like she believed him.

The clock ticked slowly. Sam didn't think she could wait much longer to see Mike. She was ready to jump out of her skin. Jake put his arm around her, and it settled her somewhat. Jake wasn't her Dom, but his instinct to soothe and protect his friend's sub was evident, and Sam was grateful.

Derek's arrival served as a welcome distraction. Cassie watched him warily as he entered, but the minute he saw her, he lit up. Cassie ran to him.

"Oh, Daddy, I'm so sorry. I made such a mess of things." She began to cry in her father's arms.

Derek stood holding her without speaking. Sam thought he would squeeze her to death, his hold on her was so tight. Finally he looked at Cassie, tears streaming down his face. It was touching that this massive, well-built soldier was brought to tears by his daughter.

"Hey, sweetheart, it's going to be all right. Mike will be okay and you're back with your family. Nothing else is important right now."

He kissed Cassie's head and squeezed her tightly once more. After a few moments of enjoying the safety of her father's arms, she pulled herself from his grasp.

Without looking up at him, she apologized again. Derek lifted her chin so she would see his face.

"Your apology is accepted. But I need your word that you won't go back to that guy. Ever!" The vehemence in his voice made her jump.

"I promise. I can't imagine going back there." The tears started to fall again.

Derek wrapped his burly arms around his little girl. "Let's go home. Your mother and sisters can't wait to see you."

He turned and thanked Jake for calling him, then told Sam he'd keep in touch to find out when he could come see Mike.

"I'll let you know," Sam promised. "He's supposed to come home tomorrow."

"Great. I'll be over as soon as he comes home."

Derek and Cassie left, and Sam settled back into the comfort of Jake's arms. They sat in silence, and before long, she dozed off.

* * * *

Mike woke to the beeping of machinery all around him. He took a mental assessment of his condition, determining that aside from the dull ache in his shoulder, he was okay. Getting up, however, proved more difficult than he anticipated. Dizziness assaulted him the minute he raised his head.

Where is everyone? He needed to get a hold of Sam to let her know he was fine. Well, maybe not fine, but at least he was in one piece. He tried to shout out 'hello', to get someone to come, but all he could manage was a whisper. Luckily, a nurse walked in as he tried to speak again.

"Well, hello, Mr. Lyons. I'm glad to see you're awake."

"Where's Sam?" Mike whispered.

"I'm not sure, but I'll look into it. As soon as we see how you're doing."

The nurse popped a thermometer into Mike's mouth and checked on the bags of fluid hanging from the poles next to the bed. A vision of Sam hanging from one of the poles flashed through his head, making him smile.

"What am I missing?" the nurse asked as she checked the thermometer. "You have an absolutely wicked look on your face."

Caught. Well, he didn't care. All he cared about was seeing the real Sam, not the fantasy, standing next to the bed.

"Please, find Sam."

"I definitely will. I want to see the woman who put that look on your face."

She finished entering notes on an iPad, placed it at the foot of his bed and left. It seemed like an eternity, but finally Sam entered the room followed by Jake. He tried to rise to greet her, but another wave of dizziness assailed him. He could only give her a wan smile.

Sam sat down next to the bed and tentatively took his hand. She brushed soft kisses over the top and he felt a reassuring stir of his cock. He was going to be fine.

"Hey, my gorgeous girl, it's so good to see you," he croaked.

Teardrops cascaded down her cheek, wetting his hand as she continued to kiss him. Jake began to stroke her back and Mike was shocked by his Neanderthal response. He wanted to kill him. Jake retreated as he watched Mike's face.

"Sorry, buddy, just trying to help," Jake reassured him.

"I know. I'm feeling a bit possessive now that I have her here," Mike explained.

"Believe me, I get it."

Sam was completely oblivious to the male one-upmanship going on around her. Mike cupped her cheek to wipe away some of the tears. The liquid welling up in Sam's eyes broke his heart.

"I'm okay. It's just my shoulder, and I'm sure I'll be back at work in no time."

"That's what I'm afraid of. I almost lost you! I don't know if I can go through this again."

She collapsed against the low side rail, hiding her face from him.

"Sam, look at me. Right now."

Even in a whisper, his Dom voice stirred her. She raised her head and met his gaze.

"It will be okay. I promise. Now give me a kiss right here," he said, pointing to his lips. "It's been way too long since I've tasted your sweetness."

Obediently, she leaned over to give him a gentle kiss. He could tell from her tentative approach that she was afraid to hurt him. He'd show her how wrong she was.

Placing his palm on the back of her head, he drew her to him and firmly held her while he plundered her mouth. Her answer was a desperate whimper. She allowed him complete access, and he took full advantage.

All of a sudden the nurse came flying back into the room. Her disapproving *tsk* wasn't enough to make him stop, but her admonition that he was doing himself harm did catch his attention.

"Your blood pressure is becoming elevated, Mr. Lyons. This is not a good idea. You should stop right now before it gets any more serious."

Mike looked up at the nurse through wisps of Sam's hair. He didn't want to let go, but maybe he'd have to slow down to keep the nurse from doing anything drastic. He released his hold on Sam's head and she sat up, her face beautifully flushed, by passion or embarrassment at being caught he wasn't sure.

"Sorry to disturb you," he addressed the nurse. "We'll be good...for now."

"I hope so. What you do when you get out of here is your own business. But under my watch, you'll behave."

"Yes, ma'am," he said and saluted her. She smiled and left the room. Jake's laugh resounded against the walls.

"You better get yourself well and out of here or your reunion with Sam is going to be severely curtailed."

"You're absolutely right." Mike winked at Sam. "I'm going to do my best. I need to have some quality time with my girl."

"You're going to rest so you can heal properly. I'm not letting you push yourself," Sam warned.

"Hey, who's the Dom around here?" Mike protested.

"Until you're up and about, I'm giving the orders." A look of determination flashed over her face.

Holding his hands up in surrender, Mike gave over his control...for now. "Okay, my girl, you win. But just be careful. Any disrespect will be dealt with once I'm better."

"You've got a ways to go before your arm is ready for a full swing. I'll worry about it when the time comes."

"I'm good enough to be able to record a list of transgressions."

Sam leaned forward and gave him a solid but chaste kiss. "I'll only kick your ass when you need it. And I'll be more than ready for you to beat mine when you're up to it."

"You got a date," he promised.

Jake cleared his throat. "I think I'll leave you two and get back to my own girl waiting for me at home. Glad you're doing well, Mike. I'll check in tomorrow."

"Thanks for everything. Say hi to Mya for me," Sam said.

"I will."

Sam got up and hugged him.

"If you need anything, just call." Jake told her.

"Thanks. I'll keep you updated." She gave him a quick peck on the cheek, and Jake left.

"Alone at last." Mike waggled his eyebrows.

"Down, boy. It will be a while before we need privacy."

"C'mere. At least let me hold you."

Sam sank into his arms, tears once again welling up.

"Hey, I'm good. Or I will be," he assured her.

"You better be." She swatted him gently on the chest.

"That's one," he said gleefully.

Chapter Ten

Two weeks of rest and Mike was already back at work despite Sam's and the visiting nurse's insistence that he wait longer. The wound was healing nicely, but it still needed tending, and Sam was furious Mike wasn't listening to her. He'd promised her he wouldn't go out into the field, but she was still worried he would screw up the healing process. But the more his wound healed, the less he allowed her to order him around. His dominance was so ingrained it was impossible for him to truly let go and allow her to take care of him.

Sam waited for him to get home, anxious to see how his first day back went. She had prepared a dinner of his favorite meatballs and spaghetti. She conceded that he was never going to learn how to cook. He didn't have the patience and having a ready-made chef in the house took away all his incentive. And on the nights she worked late, he made do with leftovers or his customary takeout.

It was okay. It had never been her intention to change him. He suited her in all the right ways, but this situation was a challenge. She felt as protective of him as he was of her, and she was having a hard time making him understand.

Hearing Mike's key turn in the lock, Sam churned with excitement, but she restrained herself from rushing to the door to greet him. She wanted him to know she was angry.

She nonchalantly brought dishes and silverware to the table and began to set it, though she was keenly aware of what he was doing. When she returned to the kitchen, he followed her and grabbed her around the waist.

"Smells delicious in here, my lovely girl. Between you and the food I don't know what smells better. I guess I don't have to choose. I can enjoy it all."

He nuzzled her neck and she wanted to melt into him, but her anger kept her body stiff and unyielding. Mike didn't try to coax her out of it. He dropped back and just stood there while she continued to go about her business.

"I need to know," he finally asked, "how long before you stop being angry at me?"

Sam turned on him. "How long before you stop being an ass and start taking care of yourself properly? That long."

Mike's raised eyebrows stopped her rant. They stood there in a standoff for what seemed like an eternity. Her heart pounding, Sam waited for Mike's response, feeling a mixture of fury and apprehension.

At last he spoke, his voice carefully controlled. "Do you see this scar that runs across my throat and down my chest?"

"Of course," she whispered, unable to speak normally through the dread at what he was going to tell her.

"I lay in a hospital for weeks, incapable of moving or speaking or even thinking with all the drugs they pumped into me for the excruciating pain. I fought back from that and healed and made myself almost as good as new through intense physical and psychological therapy. You will have to trust that I know my limits. And you will *never* speak to me in that tone again. Do I make myself clear?"

His voice had taken on a stern tone. Though she knew he would never hurt her, she realized that she'd pushed him too far.

"I'm sorry. I've just been so worried about you. I saw what happened when Mya's friend got shot and it seemed like she was okay and then *she died!*" Sam took a deep breath to calm herself. Yelling wouldn't help. "I don't know what I'd do if that happened to you," she choked out, unable to keep her tears from cascading down her cheeks.

He held out his arms and in an instant she was squeezed tightly to his chest.

"I'm not hurt like Sadie was," he reassured her. He cupped her chin to force her to look at him. "It won't happen to me. I promise."

She relaxed against him. "It better not," she warned, her words of false bravado not fooling either of them.

Mike stroked Sam's back in an effort to calm her and bring her back from the brink of hysteria. He hadn't associated the trauma of Sadie's dying with the way Sam was treating his injury. Now that he understood, he was almost willing to let her temper tantrum slide.

She hadn't been around the horrors of wartime like he had to realize that a clean shot through the shoulder was nothing compared to the damage he could have had. But she also had to learn that yelling at him and withholding her affection were not ways to get his attention. She needed to communicate her needs, and her fears, in the proper manner.

For now, he wanted to deflect her mood. Squeezing her ass cheeks as he lifted her up against him encouraged her to wrap her legs around him, taking the pressure off his shoulder. He nuzzled her neck, and this time she melted against him, all soft and compliant.

"Are we skipping dinner again, Sir?"

"I think we can wait till after. But once you serve everything, I want you naked."

She smiled coyly, a look he didn't see on her often. She lifted her chin, seeking a kiss, lips slightly parted, a hair's breadth from his own, offering herself to him. Plundering her mouth, he reasserted his control, assuring her of his strength and reminding her of his passion. She clung to him, pressing herself along his torso, letting him have his way while freely expressing her own desire. He could have devoured her right there against the kitchen cabinets, but he stopped himself. Her distressed moan told him she would have let him.

"Okay, my greedy girl, let's satisfy one hunger before we move on to the next. Get down, get dinner on the table, get naked."

She nipped him on the neck just before she slid down his body, copping a feel of his crotch before she walked over to the stove.

"Don't think I won't remember you taking that liberty after dinner."

"I'm counting on it." A saucy smile accompanied her statement.

"Uh-huh. We'll see how much you like it later." His raised eyebrows elicited only a laugh, not the tinge of apprehension he was looking for. Okay. She'd have to wait to see that his injury didn't keep him from effectively punishing her.

As soon as everything was on the table, he went to the living room, grabbed a pillow from the couch and dropped it next to his chair. She was almost naked. He silently watched till every stitch of clothing was gone then pointed to the pillow.

"Sit. I'm going to feed you."

She stifled a groan but couldn't contain the eye roll.

"Just because I've been injured and you've been taking care of me doesn't change our dynamic. It would be a shame to see your bratty behavior resurface. I won't tolerate it, and you won't be happy with my response."

He grabbed her nipples, pinching them hard as he brought her down to the pillow, his expression uncompromising. She got the point.

"Sorry, Sir," she gasped, massaging her nipples once he released them. At the shake of his head, she let go and put her hands on her thighs, leaning forward a bit as though she could assuage the pain. Placing his hand lightly against her breastbone, he pushed her back into correct alignment. She had the good sense to keep her eyes down.

"Now that's perfect. You'll stay like that through dinner."

Her "Yes, Sir" was barely audible, but he accepted it. Sitting down, he served himself a plentiful plate of food and began to eat.

"Wow, Sam. These are terrific, even better than my mother's," he declared as he ate one of her succulent meatballs.

A proud smile graced her countenance. "You better not let your mother hear that," she admonished.

"Of course not. It will be our secret. Here, your turn."

She dutifully opened her mouth, allowing him to pop in a bit of meatball, and she groaned in appreciation.

"Good, right?" he asked.

"Yup. I've worked hard to perfect these babies, and I'm proud of them."

He unconsciously patted her head, then hesitated as he remembered the last time he'd done that. This time she seemed unfazed, nuzzling up against his hand as he drew it down her face. *Holy crap!* They'd made a lot of progress since the first time they'd played.

Dinner proceeded quietly as Sam accepted his offerings of her food, even when he licked sauce off her chin. It was a simple but decadent meal, satisfying his hunger for food and heightening his hunger for her, particularly when she remained seated after dinner waiting for his instructions.

"I'll help you clean up later. Please rise and follow me to the bedroom."

He put out his hand to help her, and with his assistance she rose gracefully, keeping her head down.

"Good girl. Now let's go."

He turned and left the kitchen with her at his heels. When they reached the bedroom, he instructed her to lie face down on the bed with her legs touching the floor. Once she got into position, he kicked open her legs so that she was spread to his view. He sat down next to her and ran his hands up and down her back, every so often caressing her ass.

"We have some unfinished business, don't we?" he asked.

She attempted to rise up but he pressed her down. "I'm not sure what you mean, Sir." She sounded genuine.

"Well, let's see... Yelling at me instead of talking with me sensibly about your concerns about my health with a side of bratty behavior."

"I thought you already took care of the bratty behavior. My nipples sure thought so," she complained.

"That was a preventive measure to make sure you didn't dig yourself any deeper, my naughty girl. But despite your apprehension about my injury, which I understand, you've crossed the line on more than one occasion with bad behavior. This stops now. So, as you have so rightly pointed out, I have to be careful with my arm. That means I need something that won't take too much effort on my part to make my point. What do you think I could use to accomplish that?"

He patted her ass as he spoke.

"I don't know, Sir."

"I think you do, but you don't want to mention it in case that's not what I'm thinking. It is, so tell me yourself."

A whimper escaped her lips before she uttered the word "Cane."

"That's right. I'll go get it and we'll take care of this punishment. I want to get to the fun part."

"Sadist that you are, I think punishment is the fun part for you."

"I think you're right. But I believe you have another feeling about it, don't you?"

She mewled in response, her ass cheeks clenching protectively. He patted them again.

"Relax. It will hurt way more if you keep those yummy cheeks all tightened up."

He gave her a solid smack before he got up to fetch the cane. On his return, he pressed his body over hers and lightly bit down on her earlobe. She shivered.

"I'm just going to give you five, but they will be solid. You don't have to count. When it's over, we start fresh. But I'm warning you. I will never be fine with bratty behavior, and next time it will be much worse. Am I clear?"

Fuck! A serious caning hurt like hell with no mitigating erotic elements for her. Unlike the game they'd played, when he'd been gentle with his strokes, even five strokes were going to be hard to take. It was all she could do to relax, and it worried her. It would hurt a lot more if she were tense.

The tapping of the cane against her ass deflected her from her fearful musings.

"I asked you a question, Sam. Am I clear?"

"Yes, Sir," she responded quickly, not wanting to make the punishment worse.

"Ask me."

She didn't need him to clarify. She knew the drill. She just hadn't had to follow it in a long, long time. It took her a moment to remind herself that this was Mike, the Dom she could trust, the Dom who wouldn't abuse her. She deserved this punishment and she needed to own up to it.

"Please, Sir, I need to be punished for my bad behavior."

"Yes, Sam, you do. Five strikes and it's over."

She closed her eyes and waited, heart pounding, breath shallow. He gently stroked her back, her ass.

"Breathe slowly," he instructed.

She allowed herself to be lulled by his gentle caresses and soft words. Then came the first strike, a line of fire causing her to cry out with the aftershock, feeling as though the force was going down to the bone. Her whole body stiffened against the searing pain, her nails digging into her palms, her legs tense, her toes curled.

"Ssshhh, Sam. Inhale deeply," he coaxed. Again he smoothed his hands over her skin, helping her relax. Only this time she couldn't totally calm down, knowing what was coming.

The second strike landed just under the first, another line of fire searing her tender skin. The following aftershock took her breath away, her mouth forming a voiceless 'O'. She began to shake her head no to any more.

"You can do it, my brave girl. I know you can."

His soothing hands only exacerbated her dread, knowing they were a subterfuge, the calm before the storm.

He carefully placed the third strike below the second and she rolled over before he could stop her, glaring at him while her hand unsuccessfully tried to massage away the pain. He didn't move, meeting her gaze with the steel of his own, his determination to finish the punishment evident in his implacable expression.

It was a turning point and she knew it. He had never punished her before. If they were going to work, she had to truly submit, even when she hated it. It wasn't the pain. She was a pain slut, after all. This might not be her particular kink, but she could certainly bear it. It was her choice. If she chose to opt out now, it would be over…forever. Mike was not the kind of Dom who was ambivalent about discipline and protocol — he expected respect and obedience. This punishment was also an ultimatum. Submitting to his discipline was acceptance of his control in their relationship.

She admitted to herself this was what she wanted, what she needed. He grounded her, challenged her, pushed her to become more. If she safeworded now, she would lose the best thing that ever happened to her. Lowering her eyes, softening her expression, Sam rolled back into position. She opened her fists, spread out her fingers and took a deep breath.

"I apologize for stalling. I'm ready to continue, Sir," she told him, her voice strong with conviction.

Mike took a deep breath himself, as though he had been waiting for her to safeword. He watched her for a moment before he nodded and squared his shoulders.

The next strike fell swiftly in line with the rest, with no concession to her acquiescence. Despite the blistering pain Sam held her position, but she couldn't hold back another sob.

"Just one more and you're done. Breathe for me," he instructed.

Her breath choppy, she closed her eyes and softened against the bed. The final swat hit at the tender junction of her buttocks and thighs, the ultimate declaration of his dominance and her submission. Unable to control the tears, she sobbed into the quilt, a release of the pain and loneliness of her former life.

Mike scooped her up and sat against the headboard, cradling her in his arms.

"Hey, my beautiful girl, I'm so proud of you. You did well."

He rained kisses on her head, her face, her neck. She sobbed silently, unable to stop the cathartic tears.

It's over, thank God. He hated to cause her pain she didn't crave, but he also couldn't allow her to run over him. He respected her strength, her competence, her ability to take care of herself and others. She was a leader in the kitchen and her friends turned to her for support. But there was a line he couldn't allow her to cross, and he had to make sure she didn't step over it again or there would be real trouble in their relationship. After all he'd been through, he needed peace in his life. He believed she did too.

Sam stopped crying, nuzzling up against him as though she wanted to crawl inside him. He squeezed her tighter, sandwiching her between his legs so she would feel surrounded by him. She needed to feel protected, and he needed her to know he would provide that safe place for her.

They lay entwined in each other, her breaths tuned to his in perfect synchrony. Closing his eyes, he drank in the serenity of her closeness, her softness, her surrender. They were going to work, and he didn't remember the last time he'd been this contented…and happy.

They must have dozed off, because the next thing he knew she was placing gentle kisses along his neck and down his chest, tracing the line of his scar.

"I can't believe what you went through. I'm so grateful you're a fighter, that you got better and I can be here with you."

"You're my greatest reward, my beautiful girl."

He returned the kisses, tracing down her forehead, over her eyes, along her cheeks as she raised her head to allow him access. By the time he reached her mouth his kisses became more insistent, filled with the need to claim her. She opened herself to him fully, pliant in his arms.

He pressed her into the bed, capturing her hands above her head. She parted her legs, inviting him in. He desperately wanted to feel her warm flesh against his own without a barrier between them.

"I'm clean, Sam."

"I am too, and I'm on birth control. Please..."

She didn't need to say another word. He plunged inside her, unable to be gentle. She rose to meet his thrusts, a desperation of her own evident in her wild movements. Their heavy breathing, the slapping of their bodies crashing into each other, her moans accelerating into a keening cry drove him to completion faster than he'd intended, but he couldn't hold back from her any longer. As he emptied himself inside her, he felt complete at last.

They lay there panting until he realized his full weight was on her. He rolled them over but kept them joined with his arms around her. He wasn't ready to release her yet despite the slight twinge of pain he felt from his injury. She settled herself, allowing her spread legs to lie alongside his own as she rested her head on his chest. He loved that she didn't squirm away from letting him feel the whole weight of her on top of him, letting him support her.

He kissed the top of her head and she smiled against his chest.

"What's so funny?"

"Not funny...happy. I could lie like this forever."

"I almost could too. But that would mean we wouldn't play again or fuck or make love."

She gazed up at him with a look of confusion. "What's the difference between fucking and making love?"

"I hope you'll learn the difference soon. That sometimes as your Dom I'll use you, my little pain slut, for my own pleasure without regard to yours. That's fucking. But mostly, when we come together I need to give *you* pleasure, to connect not just with your body but with your soul. Like we did now. Did you not feel it?"

"Yes. To the very depths of my being. It's why I feel so content now."

"You know that contentment comes from love." He squeezed her tight. "I love you, Sam."

Tears welled up in her eyes despite her smile. "I love you too, Mike. With all my heart." The tears escaped down her cheek and she chuckled. "Happy tears, I promise," she assured him as he wiped them away with his thumbs.

"I hope so, beautiful girl. It will be my goal in life to make you happy. I just hope I don't have you crying all the time."

She returned his crooked grin with one of her own. "You don't know girls at all, do you?" she teased.

He got serious as he ran his hands down her body. "I've never known a girl like you. And I've never loved any girl like I love you. So be patient. I'm still learning."

"You can have all the time you need. I'm not going anywhere," she promised as she snuggled against him.

Good. Very, very good.

Epilogue

Mike's shoulder had healed to the point where he could practice his dragontail skills. Sam walked into the bedroom just as he shredded his paper target.

"How many times did you have to strike that before it disintegrated?" she asked.

"Enough to shred your beautiful ass," he answered with a smirk.

"My ass is ready any time you want to play, Sir."

It was actually more than ready. Despite the beauty of the making love part of their relationship, something they were doing often, she yearned to once again play with him in the dungeon.

He motioned for her to approach and she went to him eagerly. He encircled her in his arms.

"I didn't want to play till I was sure I was competent. My greatest fear would be to hurt you unintentionally. But I feel ready now. We're going to the Playground tonight. I want you to wear the same red corset outfit you wore the first time we played. I'll never forget how beautiful you looked in it." A playful swat on her ass emphasized his point.

She leaned into him, a mischievous look on her face. "I think it turned you on more than you expected. Kind of pushed your sense of control a bit."

"I'm not ashamed to admit it, beautiful girl. You were so delectable it took effort for me not to fuck you silly once you took your skirt off." He gave her another playful swat. "This time I'll be prepared for that vision in red."

"Good. Because I need to play hard. I've missed your taking me over completely, removing all my defenses and cracking me open."

"Don't worry. I'll do that and more. Come, let's have dinner so we have enough time to shower and get ready for tonight."

"Yes, Sir," she answered, trying to control the butterflies in her stomach. *Finally!*

* * * *

The club was packed when they arrived. Sam was so turned on already she was concerned they might have to wait a long time before they played. Mike had tortured her in the shower, making her give him a blowjob but not allowing her to get off even after he soaped her up, toying with her nipples and her clit. Now she was walking around without underwear, hoping to keep her excitement from dripping down her legs.

While they talked with friends, Mike dipped his hand under her skirt and massaged her ass, squeezing her cheeks now and again. He knew what he was doing, continuing to heighten her desire, her craving for more.

She restrained herself from expressing her discontent, not wanting to push him into punishing her rather than having a play session.

As a St. Andrew's cross became available, Sam pointed it out in the hopes that Mike would leave their friends and take her over there. He wouldn't cave to even her most gentle urging.

"When I decide, Sam," he told her, a tone of warning in his voice. "Show me your patience, your submission."

Submission she had, patience not so much. Clearly he was having fun edging her, keeping her revved up but not allowing her any relief from the hunger swirling inside her. He wrapped his arm around her shoulder and reached into her corset, giving her nipple a pinch.

"Settle down, greedy girl, or this session won't go the way you want it to."

She *was* greedy. She wanted to feel his lash scoring her body, setting it aflame. She wanted him inside, quenching the ardor he ignited every time he touched her. She had to dig deep not to squirm against his continued tormenting of her nipple, every fiber of her being burning with desire. She looked away, knowing she was unable to keep her neediness from reflecting in her eyes.

He chuckled beside her. "Good move, but don't think I'm not aware of how you're feeling right now. It will only make it better when we play."

"And that will be when, Sir?"

His raised eyebrows prevented her from asking for more clarification. *Fine.* She'd show him such patience he'd feel like she'd left the room.

Steeling herself against his touch, she took a deep breath and relaxed all her muscles. Hmm. What song should she pick to keep her mind off his persecution of her tender nipples? The nonsense of the chorus of *Hey Jude* came to mind, and singing it over and over was starting to work...somewhat.

Finally...*finally!* Mike leered at her and said, "It's time."

She grabbed him, kissed him smack on the lips and cried, "Thank God," causing him to laugh out loud, attracting the attention of their friends.

"Let us in on the joke," Ethan prompted.

"My girl here is overeager for our play session and can barely contain herself."

The knowing smiles of her friends were almost irritating, but she wasn't going to let them spoil her excitement.

Mike had her kneel at the St. Andrew's cross while the previous player wiped it down. She closed her eyes, allowing herself to enjoy the anticipation of the coming scene, getting into the proper headspace to receive the pain Mike would gift her with. When she felt Mike's hand on her head, a sign he was ready to begin, she was prepared.

"Let's get this corset and skirt off you."

He helped her rise and loosened the laces in the back of the corset so she could unhook the front. He took it from her then drew her against him, palming her breasts. She nestled her head against his hard chest, opening herself up further to his touch. He brought one hand up against her neck, squeezing against it just enough to feel as though he could stop her breathing if he wanted. She relaxed into him, letting him know she was willing to give him control over her very breath if he desired. But he didn't go any further. Instead he turned her to him and claimed her mouth in a kiss that rendered her breathless. When he pulled back, cradling her face in his hands, he stared intently into her eyes.

"You're mine now, aren't you, Sam?"

She didn't hesitate for a second before she answered, "Oh my God, yes, Sir."

He trailed his fingers down her face, cupping her chin to hold her fast while he planted a tender kiss on her lips. Then, with a look of mischief, he demanded, "Drop the skirt. I want to see all that is mine."

She stepped back, turned, unzipped the latex garment and slowly pushed it down her legs, exposing herself to him fully.

"Grab your ankles and stay right there," he directed.

She almost broke position when she felt his tongue exploring her slit, nearly sending her over before she acquired his permission.

"Please, Sir, may I come?"

"Yes," he said as he wrapped one arm tightly around her thighs, entered her with his tongue and pinched her clit. She detonated, flying apart, the only thing keeping her upright his arm securing her against him. By the time she came down, she was sitting in his lap on the floor.

Mike allowed Sam a few moments to catch her breath before helping her up. She had no idea how delightful she was when she let go, surrendering to his lead to achieve fulfillment. But he wasn't finished with this ride. They had a long way to go and he was going to take her on a trip through pleasure and pain that he hoped would bond her to him forever.

He secured her to the cross with leather cuffs then took his time exploring her. As he smoothed his hands over her tender skin, sometimes stopping to pinch a particularly inviting spot, Sam purred under his ministrations. Once he had her squirming, he began to strike her, softly at first, then harder, working to prepare her skin for the dragontail. She swayed, causing him to smile as he remembered the first time they'd played. How compliant she was now, giving herself to him without reservation, displaying a trust he was honored to have.

"Okay, my beautiful girl, it's time to be still." He kissed her neck and moved back, picking up the bullhide flogger. She murmured her pleasure, sinking into the cross, resting her head on her arm and closing her eyes. When she was pinkened to his satisfaction, he laid down the flogger and pressed against her, checking in.

"Are you good, Sam?"

"Very, Sir."

"I want you to relax and take the pain of the singletail for me now. I know this isn't your favorite, but I want you to endure for me. Can you do that?"

She leaned back toward him. "I'll take whatever you give me, Sir."

"That's my little pain slut," he told her, hugging her tight for a moment before he stepped back and picked up the singletail. He knew she preferred the dragontail, with its firm strike. The singletail stung more, annoying its victims until they could figure out how process the pain.

He settled into his stance, swirling the whip till he had a perfect rhythm, then slowly moved forward till he was grazing her shoulders. They rose, the tension in her muscles evident.

"Relax, Sam. Give over to it."

It took her a few moments, but then her shoulders dropped and she settled into a serene position. Her skin marked exquisitely, the thin red stripes covering her back, ass and thighs in a sublime testament to her submission. Humbled by her gift, he dropped the whip and once again pressed himself against her, raining gentle kisses over the imprints of his lash.

"What a good, good girl you are. I'm so proud of you."

Her breath hitched and he realized she was crying.

"Fuck! I'm taking you down."

Her cry of "Nooo!" stopped him.

"Please, not yet."

"Then tell me now. Why are you crying?" He hugged her to him, waiting.

"God, you're so bad at this part. Women cry for happiness as well as sorrow, remember?"

His laugh caused her to tense.

"Why are you laughing at me?" she demanded.

"You're not so great at this part either. Men laugh when they are relieved, when they are so happy they can't contain themselves."

He swiped at the tears on her cheek, kissed her gently over her beautiful face then asked, "Are you ready for your favorite?"

Her face lit up like a kid's on Christmas morning. "Absolutely."

"Okay, my beautiful pain slut, here we go."

He pulled back and picked up the dragontail. Once again he practiced before he landed the first stroke on her ass. A matching blow on her other cheek caused her to cry out softly, the beatific look on her face confirming her pleasure. He achieved a comfortable rhythm, which he knew would allow her to settle into the pain and absorb it in a way that would ultimately allow her to fly. Eventually she became silent, and he knew she was on her way. But it wasn't what he intended for her ultimate pleasure.

Approaching her on the cross, he caressed her and asked, "Are you okay if I turn you around?"

She smiled beatifically and nodded, so he proceeded to unhook her and rehook her facing out.

Sam closed her eyes as he raised the whip and struck her right on the nipple. The crack of pain transmuted to exhilarating pleasure in an instant. She was in the zone, the pain a vehicle transporting her to subspace, a high where all her senses were alive and all she could do was feel.

Crack! Her left nipple exploded in delicious pain, her body inching forward, seeking more. *Crack! Crack! Crack!* Delirious in a profusion of sensations, every nerve ending fired up, Sam cried out, her exhilaration building.

The next strike hit her clit, leaving her dangling on the edge of bliss until the following strike sent her over screaming, intoxicated by euphoria. The whip continued to strike, carrying her along in wave after wave of ecstasy until her body collapsed, unable to go on.

Mike held her securely while someone else released her from her bonds. He lifted her up and carried her to a couch, where he wrapped her in a blanket and pressed a bottle of water to her lips. She didn't even realize how dehydrated she was until the water slid over her parched lips, reviving her senses. She curled up into the shelter of his arms, content to let his warmth envelop her. She drifted without much thought or concern. She had never felt so safe, so protected, so cherished.

She had no idea of time, how long she rested in Mike's embrace before he asked, "Hey, how are you doing?"

Sam smiled up at him. "I'm good, Sir. I'm still coming down. That was an incredible scene."

"Would you like to adjourn to a private area for the make-love portion of the scene?" Mike stared at her with longing, his desire for her to accept his offer of love clear in his expression.

Sam knew this was it. She was ready to return Mike's love in every way he gave it to her, to open her heart to him without hesitation. "Yes, my darling Sir, I'd love to adjourn to the make-love portion of the evening."

His face lit up. He immediately rose, carrying her with him as he made his way to one of the private rooms of the club, only stopping to grab his toy bag. Once he closed the door, he set her on her feet.

"I'd like you to kneel for me, my beautiful girl, before we do anything else."

Sam slid to her knees, ready to show him exactly how submissive she felt. Mike reached into his bag, pulling out a long box, which he then opened, taking out a heavy silver chain with a large heart secured in the middle, inscribed 'Forever Mine'. The chain released from the heart with a key, and as Mike unlocked it, he looked down at Sam.

"I love you, Sam…I cherish you…I need you…I want you. I promise to love you with all my heart, to protect you with all my being, to care for you always. Will you wear my collar?"

Sam's tears ran down her face despite the smile she couldn't repress. "Happiness," she informed him as he wiped the wetness from her cheeks. "I would be proud to wear your collar, to show the world I belong to the best man I know, to the man I love more than anything."

She pulled her hair up so Mike could secure the collar around her neck, its weight bringing a serenity over her she didn't know existed. He extended his hand and helped her rise, then enveloped her in an almost painfully tight hug while he kissed her breathless. She melted into his embrace, finally feeling like she was home.

When he came up for air, Mike told her, "I didn't make this a public collaring ceremony because I know you like to keep your feelings private. I hope I made the right choice."

"You did. As much as I love my friends, I couldn't bear the look of triumph on Rebecca's face when you locked this around my neck. It is too momentous an occasion for me to be distracted by anyone else's feelings about it. I promise to let her feel superior later. She earned it. I also don't want to wait for people to congratulate us before we get to the make-love portion of the evening."

Mike's joyous laugh was infectious, causing her to laugh along with him as he pulled her to the bed. She sighed as he secured her arms and legs to the bedposts, happy that she had found the man who could dominate her so totally. She would never have to endure vanilla sex again or the censure of a man who didn't understand her cravings. Mike would always ensure that the make-love portion of the evening allowed her to follow her kink to ultimate bliss. *How did I get so lucky?*

By the time Mike entered her, she was overwhelmed with need, desperate to connect in every way with this amazing man she could now call her own.

"Please...don't hold back, Sir."

"I couldn't if I wanted to. You drive me crazy, Sam. I can't seem to get enough of you." He emphasized his statement with powerful thrusts right to her core, melding with her, claiming her, possessing her. She was finally free to let go, trusting that she was safe in his arms.

"Come with me, my beautiful girl," he demanded when he realized she was at the pinnacle of pleasure, and she tumbled over with him, perfectly in sync as she gave him all she had.

Want to see more from this author? Here's a taster for you to enjoy!

His Domain

The Auction

Rose C. Carole

Excerpt

Jenna stood looking at the scraps of fabric that were supposed to be her outfit for the evening and sighed. There was no way around it. David had been so excited when he'd spied the outfit on a mannequin in the flea market. But the mannequin had represented a size six, so when the elaborate scarves with the metal bells — which were supposed to go around the waist of a belly dancer so they jangled when she danced — had been draped around the figure like a bikini, one for the top and one for the bottom, it had looked beautiful. But Jenna wasn't a size six — she was more like a sixteen. At least she had been able to convince David that she needed two scarves for each piece.

Jenna tied the first two scarves together and wrapped them around her waist. The front wasn't too bad. Thankfully it came to the tops of her thighs and covered her completely. But the back allowed her ass cheeks to peek from below, and there was no way David was going to allow her panties, so she was going to be flaunting her backside. Oh well, of all her features to be exposed, she was more comfortable with that one.

The top was a bit tricky. Her ample breasts were hard to contain when she pulled the scarves from around her back up over her breasts and tied them like a halter top. This was not like a bra, holding her in securely. She would have to be careful that the top stayed in place or she would slip out for all to see. *Ugh!*

She wasn't happy about this whole auction thing, anyway. It was common practice in BDSM dungeons to auction people off for play. It was a way for people to get to know one another in a fun environment, and the auctions always had a great turnout. But Jenna had never participated other than as a spectator, not wanting to put herself up there with all those cute young things who looked so tempting. It would be too embarrassing when no one bid on her. She was the type who was much better when you got to know her. It was how she'd gotten involved with David. They'd met at a munch, then for coffee a few times, and finally they'd played in the club.

Now David, who had collared her a year ago, was going to put her up for auction. She had tried to talk him out of it, but he was proud of her and wanted to show her off. He was the auctioneer so he had control over the situation. He would also be sure to supervise any play that happened after the auction—in fact, he planned to participate—and he would be careful to restrict what kind of play they would engage in. It would all be delineated on her auction application form. Despite her reluctance, he was her Dom, and as long as she wasn't in danger of getting hurt or going against her hard limits, she would do what he wanted. Truth be told , she was torn between excitement and dread.

She removed the outfit, put it in her bag and donned her street clothes for the trip to the club. The fantasy rooms that were usually closed to the members of the Lair because they were used by paid, professional Dommes were being opened for the evening. She had only seen them once before. There was a schoolroom, a medical office, a dungeon-like room with stone walls, an interrogation room and a Victorian bedroom. The biggest room was a harem room, and the auction was going to take place there.

David was waiting for her downstairs, holding his own bag with his toys and his outfit, except for his leather kilt, which was on a hanger and draped over his shoulder.

"Ready?" he asked, his voice full of anticipation.

"I guess so. I wish you would at least rethink my outfit. I feel so much better in a corset. And most of the other women will be wearing one, as well."

David sidled up to her, pressing his body against hers and kissing her softly on the cheek.

"I don't care what others are wearing. I love you in that outfit. You look so hot."

Jenna rolled her eyes at him. She could afford the disrespectful gesture since David's hands were full and he couldn't swat her ass. But she moved away from him anyway after she did it. She could never quite predict how he would react. He kept her on her toes, which made their relationship very intoxicating, even two years in. David just raised his eyebrows at her, which she knew meant, *You'll pay for that later.*

"C'mon. I don't want to be late. I have to go through all the applications for the auction and make sure I'm familiar with each person when it's their turn."

He led her out of the house. It was time to face the music.

About the Author

Rose has been an avid reader all her life and pursued that obsession into the publishing business, where she worked in both production and editorial for books and magazines. When her son went off to college, she decided to fulfill another passion and went to culinary school, thinking she would write a cookbook but loving the cooking so much she became a caterer. But her love for books is ever-present and she finally decided it was time to follow her own creative muse and write the kinds of books she enjoys reading. She hopes her readers enjoy them as well.

Rose loves to hear from readers. You can find her contact information, website details and author profile page at http://www.totallybound.com.

CPSIA information can be obtained
at www.ICGtesting.com
Printed in the USA
FSHW01n0840190618
49336FS